HONEY BUNCH:
HER FIRST WINTER
AT SNOWTOP

Trix pulled Honey Bunch up the hill.

Honey Bunch: Her First Winter at Snowtop

HONEY BUNCH:
HER FIRST WINTER
AT
SNOWTOP

By
HELEN LOUISE THORNDYKE
AUTHOR OF: HONEY BUNCH: JUST A LITTLE GIRL
HONEY BUNCH: HER FIRST TWIN PLAYMATES, ETC.

NEW YORK
Grosset & Dunlap
PUBLISHERS

CONTENTS

HONEY BUNCH:
HER FIRST WINTER
AT SNOWTOP

CHAPTER I

TOBOGGAN HILL

TING-A-LING went the telephone in the Morton home.

Honey Bunch, who had just finished dressing her doll Eleanor, listened as the bell rang a second time. She wondered if she should answer it since her mother and father were not at home. But just then Mrs. Miller, the laundress, said:

"Hello. Yes, she's here. I'll call her. Honey Bunch! Come to the phone, dear."

Honey Bunch Morton did not receive a telephone call very often and knew this one must be important. She ran down the stairs and said:

"Hello."

"Oh, Honey Bunch, this is Ida," said a little girl at the other end of the line. "What are you doing?"

"Playing with my doll Eleanor. Why?"

"My mother says she'll take us coasting on Toboggan Hill."

1

Honey Bunch jumped up and down in delight. Toboggan Hill was a wonderful place where people went sledding and skiing. There was always some very good skier to watch; sometimes it was a boy or a girl. And the ride down the hill on a sled was a long, exciting one.

"It'll be fun to go coasting there," Honey Bunch told Ida. "When are we going?"

"Right away. Bring your sled and be here in fifteen minutes," said Ida, and hung up the telephone.

Honey Bunch ran to the kitchen to find Mrs. Miller. The laundress did other work at the Morton home besides washing and ironing the clothes. She usually stayed with Honey Bunch when the little girl's parents were out. Honey Bunch liked her very much.

"Please, Mrs. Miller," she said, "may I go coasting with Ida Camp's mother?" When the laundress nodded her head "yes," the little girl went on, "I ought to wear my snowsuit and I can't get into it myself. Will you help me?"

"Yes, dear."

Before they could start upstairs to put on the snowsuit the back door opened. In came Norman Clark. He was a jolly little boy who lived back of the Mortons. Whenever he came to see Honey Bunch he climbed over the fence instead of coming around by the street. He never knocked on the door. Norman was mischievous and at times worried his parents and the Mortons very much.

As the little boy came in, Mrs. Miller frowned. "I'm sorry, Norman," she said, "but you can't stay."

"Why not?" he asked.

Mrs. Miller explained that Honey Bunch was going out in a few minutes and could not play with him. Norman asked where she was going. When he heard it was coasting in the park, he wanted to go too.

"Do you think Mrs. Camp would take me?" he asked.

Mrs. Miller thought Norman was bound to get into trouble if he went coasting, but she did not say anything.

"I'll call up and ask Ida," Honey Bunch offered kindly. "Could you be ready in fifteen minutes if she says it's all right?"

"I'm ready now," the little boy declared.

Norman did have on a heavy winter snowsuit with a cap and boots. The only things missing were gloves, but Norman rarely wore gloves anyhow.

Honey Bunch spoke to Ida on the telephone. Now, Ida did not care very much for Norman, because he had once borrowed her roller skates and left them out in the rain to rust. Another time he had thrown her hat up in a tree, and the birds had pecked holes in it so she could not wear it again. But Ida knew Norman was not really mean, and she did not wish to be mean either.

"Oh, tell him to come along," she said, after asking her mother.

Honey Bunch ran back to tell Norman the good news, and he hurried home to get his sled. She and Mrs. Miller went upstairs and got her snowsuit from the closet.

"My goodness!" said the laundress. "This suit is about on its last legs."

Honey Bunch looked up at her. "What do you mean by that?" she asked.

Mrs. Miller explained that when a thing was on its last legs it could not stand by itself any longer. Honey Bunch remarked that her snowsuit never could stand alone.

"I mean," said Mrs. Miller, laughing, "that

4

when something is about to give out and not be of use much longer, we say it's on its last legs."

Honey Bunch giggled and said, "I hope my suit will last for the rest of the winter, 'cause Mother doesn't want to buy me a new one. She says I'm growing so fast it wouldn't fit me next year."

"That's right, so you'd better take good care of your snowsuit this afternoon," said Mrs. Miller, tying the ribbons of the cap under Honey Bunch's chin.

The little girl looked very pretty. Her golden curls peeked out from beneath her cap, and her big blue eyes danced at the thought of the fun she was going to have.

Norman was waiting when she got downstairs, and together they pulled their sleds to Ida Camp's house. The Camps owned a station wagon, so several children had been invited. One by one their sleds were piled into the back of the wagon. Then the boys and girls scrambled in for seats. Mrs. Camp said her passengers would have to sit still or someone might tumble out.

"And maybe be broken to pieces like Humpty Dumpty," thought Honey Bunch.

When they neared the park, they saw many cars carrying people with skis and sleds. They were all going to Toboggan Hill.

One old car tried to pass the station wagon. It made a great deal of noise, and smoke came from the rear of it. Honey Bunch decided it must be on its last legs.

"Well, here we are at last, children," said Mrs. Camp. "Please don't get out of the car until I tell you."

She parked some distance from the hill, and made the boys and girls get out quietly and wait while she and Norman lifted out their sleds.

What a sight the hill was! It was dotted with sleds of all sizes. Gay-colored snowsuits mingled with dark ones. Some of the coasters had on hats, but others did not. Most of the men and women who were skiing wore sunglasses.

When Honey Bunch and the other children reached the coasting section, Norman was the first one to go down on his sled. He fell upon it so hard it nearly knocked the breath from him. The others laughed.

"My goodness," said Mrs. Camp, "if he does that very often he will be black and blue."

She sat down on a log to watch the children.

"Let's go down side by side," suggested Ida to Honey Bunch, "and see who gets to the bottom first."

The two little girls seated themselves on their sleds, put their feet on the steering rudders, and off they went. They reached the bottom of the hill at exactly the same moment.

"It's a funny race when you come out just the same," giggled Honey Bunch.

The two friends trudged up the hill, and then went down again on their sleds. They did this many times. Their cheeks were red as apples and their eyes sparkled like the sun dancing on water. This was such fun!

One time when Honey Bunch reached the bottom of the hill, she found herself far away from the other children with whom she had been playing. Suddenly she noticed a little girl on a sled. The sled was being pulled uphill by a big collie dog.

"Oh, what a wonderful way to get up the hill," Honey Bunch thought. "I wish I could do that."

As she watched, the dog reached the top of the hill. The little girl unhooked him, turned the sled around, and seated herself on it. Then down she came at full speed, the dog running behind and barking gleefully.

When the sled reached the foot of the hill, Honey Bunch went over to speak to the little girl. They smiled at each other, and Honey Bunch patted the big dog.

"What's his name?" she asked.

"Trix," said the other girl. "He doesn't belong to me. He lives at the house where I'm staying."

"Oh, don't you live in Barham?" asked Honey Bunch. This was the name of the town where the Mortons lived.

"No, I live far away from here near Snowtop Mountain," the little girl told her. "My daddy came to Barham on business, so he brought me along for a visit."

The child, who was dark and very pretty, said her name was Christina, and that she lived up North, where the snow was much deeper than around Barham.

"How could you get away from there," Honey Bunch asked her, "if the snow is so deep?"

"We rode to the station in a sleigh. All winter we use horses and sleds. We never use automobiles," said Christina.

8

"I'd like that," Honey Bunch remarked. "And do you have dogs that pull the sleds?"

Christina said that not far from where she lived some people had Eskimo dogs who pulled sleds, but her father did not own any.

"Would you like to ride up the hill and let Trix pull you?" she asked.

Honey Bunch said she would like this very much, and climbed onto Christina's sled. The little girl hooked Trix to it.

"Mush!" she called out, and explained this was what Eskimos said to their dogs to make them go.

Trix obediently started up the hill. Christina walked beside the sled. The two little girls chatted gaily all the way. Honey Bunch told Christina her name, and Christina told her many interesting things about her life up North. She ended by saying:

"I wish you would come to visit me sometime, Honey Bunch. My daddy and mother and my brother would love to see you."

Honey Bunch thought she would like nothing better than to go, but after she thought it over a minute she shook her head the way their laundress did.

"I'm afraid you live too far away," she said. "Mrs. Miller who works for us says we can't afford the time to go away in the winter."

At this moment Norman Clark, who had been wondering where Honey Bunch was, came over to her. He said they were going to have a race and didn't she want to be in it?

"But it's going to start right away," he told her. "We'll have to hurry. Come on!"

Honey Bunch suggested that Christina come with them, but the little girl from the North said she had to go back to the house where she was staying.

By the time both Norman and Honey Bunch reached Ida Camp and the other children, all the boys and girls were seated on their sleds, ready for the race.

"Hurry up!" one of the boys shouted.

An opening had been left in the center of the group for Honey Bunch and Norman. They got on their sleds side by side. Mrs. Camp called out "Ready! Set! Go!" and they were off!

The little boys in the group shouted and rocked back and forth to make their sleds go faster. They were sure none of the girls would win, and that really it was a race among the boys.

Some of the girls did get far behind, and two of them fell off their sleds, but Honey Bunch and Ida kept on. Halfway down the hill their sleds were even with those of three of the boys.

Then suddenly something went very wrong. Harry, who was on the left, got too far over and steered straight for Norman. Quickly Norman pulled out of the way, but he forgot all about Honey Bunch who was on the other side of him.

Crash!

He went straight into Honey Bunch's sled. Both children were thrown into the snow.

For a few seconds Honey Bunch was too stunned to get up. Then slowly she rose.

"I'm awful sorry," said Norman. "Did you hurt yourself?"

"N—no," Honey Bunch replied. "B—but look at me!"

Norman gazed at his playmate. Her snow-suit was ripped from top to bottom. She could never wear it again. Honey Bunch was afraid that without it, she would not be allowed to play in the snow any more this winter.

11

CHAPTER II

A FRIEND FROM THE NORTH

HONEY BUNCH did not blame Norman for what had happened. She knew it was an accident.

But this did not help the situation any. Honey Bunch's snowsuit, which had been "on its last legs," was ruined now. The little girl began to shiver as the wind blew through the tear in it.

"I'd better go tell Mrs. Camp," she thought.

Norman was looking downhill to see who had won the race. He was a little disgusted when he saw that Ida Camp was the winner. He had wanted to win himself. But if he couldn't, he had hoped one of the other boys might.

When Mrs. Camp saw the torn snowsuit, she said Honey Bunch must go with her to the station wagon at once. She told Norman to stay where he was until the other children came back, and to ask them to follow her right away. It

12

was some time before the children were willing
to leave Toboggan Hill, as they were having
such a wonderful time coasting.

When Honey Bunch reached her own home,
she ran inside at once. Mother and Daddy were
back and they looked at their small daughter in
amazement.

"I haven't any legs now," Honey Bunch told
them.

Mr. and Mrs. Morton wondered what she
meant. Then they laughed merrily when Honey
Bunch explained what Mrs. Miller had said
about the snowsuit being on its last legs.

"She was right," said Mrs. Morton.

Honey Bunch told her parents all about the
exciting coasting party. They were relieved
that she had not been hurt in the accident.

"I have a new friend," said Honey Bunch.
"Her name is Christina, and she had a dog
named Trix with her. He pulled her sled up
the hill, and she gave me a ride."

"How very nice," said her mother. "You say
the dog's name is Trix? I believe he belongs to
Mrs. Harden. Sometimes I see him carrying
packages home from the store for her."

Honey Bunch decided to go shopping with

her mother soon. Maybe she would see Christina and Trix at one of the stores.

"Tell me some more about your new friend Christina," said Daddy Morton.

Honey Bunch told him the little girl lived up North near Snowtop Mountain, far away from Barham, and how the snow was so deep they could not use automobiles in the winter.

"She invited me to visit her," said Honey Bunch. "But I guess I couldn't do that."

Daddy Morton looked down at his small daughter, then smiled. "You might go to visit her at that, Honey Bunch," he said.

The little girl was so surprised to hear this she did not know what to say. It sounded wonderful! But then Daddy Morton was always saying nice things and doing nice things for his family.

Honey Bunch was only a little girl, but already she had taken many trips with her daddy and mother. She had been across the country in an airplane, and out West where the cowboys lived, and only the summer before she had had her First Trip on a Houseboat. Her daddy was a lawyer, and sometimes he had to go to faraway places to see his clients. Now and then he

14

took Honey Bunch with him. She wondered if perhaps he was going to make a trip up North and take her along.

"Daddy, do you mean you know Christina?" she asked excitedly. "And I may go to visit her?"

As she said this, Honey Bunch ran across the room and climbed into her father's lap. When she had anything special to talk to her father about, she liked to sit very close to him and hold his hand. He too liked this very much.

"I don't know Christina," he replied, "but I believe she is the daughter of a man who came to my office this morning. His name is Eric Vasa. He lives up North and has a little girl named Christina."

"And has he a wife and a son?" Honey Bunch asked.

"I believe he has," Daddy Morton replied.

Mother asked why Mr. Morton thought they might go up to the man's home. Honey Bunch's father said that Mr. Vasa made beautiful jewelry by hand, and he had a very special way of getting the designs for his pieces.

"He wants to show me how he does it," said Daddy Morton. "Mr. Vasa could not explain

15

very much in my office, so he's coming here this evening to tell me more about it."

"Oh, may I stay up?" Honey Bunch asked eagerly.

"If it's not too late," her father replied. "I believe he'll bring Christina with him."

Honey Bunch jumped down from her father's lap and clapped her hands. All this sounded so exciting she could hardly wait for the callers to arrive.

At half-past seven the bell rang. She ran to the door to open it. Christina stood there, smiling.

"Father, this is Honey Bunch," she said.

"I'm glad to meet you," said Mr. Vasa in a deep voice. It made Honey Bunch think of the way wheels sound as they rumble by on the street. She decided she liked Mr. Vasa very much.

As the Vasas stepped into the hall, Mr. and Mrs. Morton came forward to greet them.

"I'm glad you didn't go to bed, Honey Bunch," said Christina. "My daddy has some things to show you."

After they were all seated in the living room, the man from the North took a large, velvet-

16

covered jewel box from his pocket. When he opened it, Honey Bunch could see several beautiful pieces of jewelry lying on a white satin lining.

"Oh!" she gasped. She never before had seen such lovely necklaces and rings and pins.

One of them was a large pin which looked like a star. Honey Bunch thought perhaps she liked this one best of all the pieces.

"They are exquisite," said Mrs. Morton. "Did you make these yourself, Mr. Vasa?"

"My daddy makes everything himself," Christina spoke up. "And he never copies other people's things like those bad men did," she added.

"What do you mean?" Honey Bunch asked her.

Mr. Vasa explained that no two of his pieces were alike, but recently he had found that some of his designs had been copied in cheap jewelry.

"They have no right to do that," he said.

"Of course not," Mr. Morton agreed.

Mr. Vasa said he wanted the lawyer to find the men who were copying the jewelry and make them stop doing it. Honey Bunch's father replied that he would do all he could.

"It's a secret where my daddy gets his designs," Christina told the Mortons.

"I should like very much to have all of you come to my home and see how it is done," Mr. Vasa said. "I'm sure my wife would like to have you." He turned to Mr. Morton and added, "I think you will understand my problem better if you see how the designs are made."

Mr. Morton thought this would be a very good idea, but Honey Bunch's mother did not feel the same way about it.

"We could not impose on you," she said. "Perhaps it would be best if Mr. Morton were to go alone."

Honey Bunch looked eagerly at her daddy to see what he would say.

"Perhaps there's a hotel near by where we could stay," he said finally. "Do you know of one?"

Mr. Vasa smiled. "Yes, there is a fine one, and you would be very comfortable there, I'm sure. It's called Snowtop Inn."

"They have lots of nice things for children to play with," Christina spoke up. "They even have a children's dining room."

"And there is a woman who plans entertainments for the little guests," added Mr. Vasa. "Yes, I think you would enjoy it at Snowtop Inn very much."

He said the hotel provided skis, skates, sleds and snowshoes for everyone, even the smallest child. Honey Bunch said she had never been on snowshoes or skis, but that she would like to try them sometime.

"There's a nice man named Rudy who teaches people how to skate and ski," Mr. Vasa told them.

Honey Bunch was so excited she could hardly sit still. Snowtop Inn sounded like just the most wonderful place in the world! She wanted to know if the Vasas went over there very often. The jeweler shook his head.

"We rarely go. I keep busy at my work, and of course Mama has many things to do. And then Christina and my son Axel have their school work and other duties."

"My brother is a wonderful skater and a wonderful dancer," Christina said proudly. "He knows all the Swedish folk dances."

"Swedish?" Honey Bunch asked.

Mr. Vasa explained that the family had come from Sweden a few years before, and that Mrs.

19

Vasa had done a great deal of dancing when she was a girl. She knew many folk dances and had taught them to her children.

Honey Bunch said she wished she might see Axel dance sometime, and asked how far away the Vasas' house was from Snowtop Inn.

"It's rather a long drive," the jeweler replied, not guessing that the little girl was already planning to go over often to play with Christina.

As she was thinking this over, Mr. Morton said to Honey Bunch's mother, "Edith, I believe it would be a good idea to have a little vacation at Snowtop. I can work on Mr. Vasa's case, while you and Honey Bunch have a good time at the hotel."

"Oh, Daddy," his small daughter cried out, running across the room to hug him. "It will be a scrumptious vacation!"

Honey Bunch liked the word scrumptious, and always used it whenever she was particularly pleased about something. Now she took Christina by the hand and ran off to the kitchen. She introduced the Vasa child to the laundress, and then added excitedly:

"We're going to Snowtop! It's way up North. The children have lots of fun there."

20

Suddenly Honey Bunch stopped smiling as an unpleasant thought came to her. Mr. Vasa had said his children did not go often to Snowtop, and that it was a long drive to their house from the hotel.

Maybe Honey Bunch would not see Christina when she was at Snowtop Inn!

CHAPTER III

THE GOING-AWAY PARTY

"CHRISTINA! Christina!" Mr. Vasa called from the front hall. "We must go now, dear."

The two little girls ran to the front of the house. Honey Bunch was sorry to say good-bye to her new-found playmate. After the Vasas had gone she told her mother what was on her mind. Mrs. Morton put her arm around her small daughter's shoulders and drew her close.

"Don't let that worry you any more, my dear," she said. "Even if Christina and Axel don't come to Snowtop Inn, we shall see them. Daddy will probably go over to their house several times and he'll take you and me with him."

Honey Bunch was relieved to hear this, and ran back to the kitchen to talk over the whole trip with Mrs. Miller. Ever since she could remember, Honey Bunch had liked to pull the kitchen stool over to the place where the laundress happened to be working and discuss everything with her. Now she pulled her special seat close to the sink and perched herself on top of it.

"I have a worry," she said. "Even if I go to Snowtop I can't play outdoors."

For a moment Mrs. Miller did not know what the child meant. Then she remembered the torn snowsuit.

"Maybe I can mend your snowsuit," she said kindly. "I'll look it over tomorrow and see what can be done."

"But it's on its last legs," said Honey Bunch. "It might burst open again and then I would freeze. It must be dreadfully cold up at Snowtop because the automobiles can't run in the wintertime."

Mrs. Miller laughed and pretended to shiver. "Give me the good old South any time," she said. "When I go on a vacation in the winter, I want to keep warm like the birds do. You know, Honey Bunch, birds have very good sense. They know enough not to stay around here when the thermometer goes down to freezing."

She began to hum a little tune and presently she sang the words to it. It was an old song about a poor bird which did not go South. It went like this:

The north wind doth blow,
We soon shall have snow,
And what will poor robin do then?
Poor thing!

Honey Bunch laughed, and said she certainly was sorry for the poor bird. She was glad she had plenty of warm clothes to take to Snowtop.

"I suppose you'll meet a great many children up there," said Mrs. Miller.

"Maybe," Honey Bunch agreed. "But I wish somebody I know could go with me. Mrs. Miller, what would you think about my cousin Stub going along?"

Mrs. Miller opened her eyes wide before she answered. She was very faithful to the Morton family and did not want to say anything against anyone in it. But Stub, who lived on a farm, often got into trouble the way Norman Clark did. Stub was only a nickname, but Honey Bunch's cousin had received it because she was always stubbing her toe and falling. She was a good-natured little girl, however, and Honey Bunch loved to have her come to visit.

Honey Bunch did not wait for the laundress to answer. She slid from the stool and ran to

24

find her mother and father. She told them her idea, and made them laugh when she promised to try to keep her small cousin from falling down so much.

"I s'pose it wouldn't look very nice at a hotel if she fell on the floor when there were lots of people around," the little girl said seriously.

Her mother remarked that this was not the worst of it. Stub seemed to have a scratch on her face and a bandage on her knee most of the time, and Mrs. Morton was always fearful the child might do herself some real harm.

"But it would be nice to have someone with you," she said. "As soon as Daddy finds out whether we can have rooms at Snowtop Inn, I'll telephone to your Aunt Carol. We'll ask her what she thinks about Stub going."

Honey Bunch had to go to bed long before the arrangements were made, but first thing in the morning she heard the good news about the trip. Two rooms would be reserved at Snowtop Inn, and her young cousin Stub would be Honey Bunch's roommate.

"Is Stub coming here or are we going to get her at the farm?" Honey Bunch asked eagerly.

She was told that Uncle Rand would drive

Stub to Barham. As soon as breakfast was over Honey Bunch asked permission to go to Ida Camp's house and tell her about their vacation at Snowtop. Suddenly she recalled her torn snowsuit.

"I guess I'll have to put on my old coat and my leggings," she said. Sighing, she added, "That's such a bother."

Her mother agreed, but said it was the only thing to do. She told her small daughter they would have to buy a new snowsuit to take to the Inn, even if Honey Bunch should outgrow it before the next winter.

"I'll get one of the waterproof kind this time," Mrs. Morton said.

Honey Bunch had seen a lovely blue one in the Kiddie Shop downtown. She told her mother about it, and asked if she might have that one if it were the right size. Mrs. Morton nodded, and said she would pick up Honey Bunch at Ida's house in half an hour. Then they would go down and try on the snowsuit.

Ida was still at the breakfast table when Honey Bunch ran in. She was so interested in hearing about her playmate's trip that she laid down her spoon. Mrs. Camp had to say "Eat

26

your cereal and drink your milk" several times before her small daughter finished her breakfast.

"When are you going?" Ida asked excitedly.

"We have to wait until Stub comes," Honey Bunch answered. "She's going with us."

Ida did not say anything for a minute. Then she turned to her mother and asked:

"May I give Honey Bunch a going-away party?"

Ida remembered the time when some friends of her parents were going on a long trip. Her mother and father had asked a lot of people to dinner to say good-bye to them. Now she thought it would be fun to invite Anna Martin and Grace Winters and Tommy Sand and some other children, maybe even Norman Clark, to come to say good-bye to Honey Bunch.

"That would be very nice," said Mrs. Camp. "Would you like a going-away party, Honey Bunch?"

"Oh, yes," cried Honey Bunch.

She was sorry she was not able to stay longer and talk more about the party, but her mother came to take her downtown to buy the new snow-suit.

"I'll see you this afternoon," Ida called as the Mortons started off.

Honey Bunch was excited over the idea of seeing all her friends before leaving Barham. Taking her mother's hand, she skipped along the street and said:

"Ida's wonderful. She's going to have a coming-off party!"

Mrs. Morton looked puzzled. "What in the world is a coming-off party?" she asked.

"For a trip," Honey Bunch answered.

"But what do you take off, and why?" asked Mrs. Morton.

Suddenly Honey Bunch realized her mistake and began to laugh. "I meant to say a going-away party," she answered.

Mrs. Morton agreed this would be fun, and the rest of the way downtown they talked about what dress Honey Bunch would wear to the party. They finally decided on a white wool with little rosebuds embroidered on it.

When they reached the Kiddie Shop, Honey Bunch pointed out the blue waterproof snow-suit. It was in the window. A clerk got it for them, and Honey Bunch tried it on.

"A perfect fit, little lady," the saleswoman

28

said. "And you look like a little bluebird in it."

"Only I haven't any wings," Honey Bunch giggled. "And I'm not going South like the birds do."

"No, you haven't any wings," the clerk laughed. "If you did, maybe the suit wouldn't fit so well."

"We'll take the suit," said Mrs. Morton. "By any chance, have you another one like it?"

She explained that Honey Bunch's cousin, who was coming to their house, was just the same size, and it might be nice for the two little girls to be dressed alike. The saleswoman found another snowsuit and wrapped up both of them.

"I hope Stub can get here in time for the going-away party," said Honey Bunch on the way home.

Ida came over later to tell her playmate that the party was planned for day after tomorrow. She also said there would be a surprise. Ida would not tell anyone what the surprise was, though.

Just before bedtime Honey Bunch's Aunt Carol telephoned to say she could not possibly get Stub ready for the trip to Snowtop in less than two days. So her little cousin would not be in Barham in time to attend the going-away party.

On the day of the party Honey Bunch walked to Ida's house with Norman. He looked very nice in a new suit, and she was very pretty in her white wool dress. They found a crowd of children on the front porch, laughing gaily.

"Why don't they go inside?" asked Norman.

In a moment he saw why. A little snowman stood there grinning at the children. Ida was saying:

"You have to shake hands with him before you come in."

Honey Bunch and Norman saw that one of the snowman's wooden arms moved up and down. One by one the little guests shook his hand and then went into the house.

"I never saw a snowman like that," said Norman, who pumped the poor fellow's arm up and down so many times that it nearly fell off. Finally Honey Bunch pulled the boy into the house.

"My father made it specially for the party," Ida Camp explained.

The children trooped into the living room where chairs had been arranged for them in a circle. Mrs. Camp told them all to sit down and said they would play a game of school. Two of the boys groaned. They were sure they were going to be asked questions about their lessons, and since they did not pay very strict attention in school, they were worried. But to their surprise Mrs. Camp, who was the teacher, said:

"Now, every time I ask you a question you must give the wrong answer. You may think this is easy, but you will find it very hard. Who wants to be first?"

Johnny Dale put up his hand. The teacher asked him how much two and two are. Johnny immediately said four. Then he laughed.

"Four is right, and you are supposed to answer wrong, aren't you?" Johnny asked.

"That's right, you're wrong," said Mrs. Camp, and everybody giggled. "Now, who's next?"

Grace Winters said, "I am," and the teacher asked her to name the colors of the American flag.

Instantly Grace answered red, white, and blue. All the children laughed and said that was right.

"But you were supposed to be wrong," said Mrs. Camp. "Now, who wants to be wrong?"

"I do!" shouted about six children together.

"Well, I'll take Norman," said Mrs. Camp. "Now pay strict attention. I never before saw so many children right. Remember, you are to answer wrong. Is water wet or dry?"

"W—e dr-r—wet!" shouted Norman.

"Well, you're almost wrong," laughed the teacher. "Oh, dear, I wish I could find someone this afternoon who could be all wrong."

Honey Bunch raised her hand. "I'll try hard, Mrs. Camp," she said.

The teacher smiled at her. "I'm going to give you a little poem, and you give me the last line. Here it is:

> *Hey, diddle, diddle!*
> *The cat and the fiddle,*
> *The cow jumped over the moon;*
> *The little dog laughed*
> *To see such sport,*
> *And the dish—*"

Honey Bunch hesitated for a second, then she laughed and said, "Danced around the room."

"Good for you!" cried Mrs. Camp, and all the children clapped their hands.

The little guests played the wrong answer game for a long time. They probably would have played nothing else, but the teacher said she had planned several other things for them. One game that Norman liked particularly was barnyard. Each child pretended to be a different animal and they all made noises at the same time. Norman was a rooster and could crow very well. As a matter of fact, he had been practicing this for a couple of years. He liked to sit on the fence between his house and Honey Bunch's and shout "Cock-a-doodle-doo" at the top of his lungs.

After the barnyard game, Norman was not so interested in what was going on. In fact, when they played Going to Jerusalem, he was the first one to lose his chair and be put out of the game. He wandered off by himself.

The little boy suddenly remembered the snowman on the front porch. He decided to go and examine its movable arm. Quietly he opened the door and went outside. Over and over Norman shook the snowman's hand. Suddenly he had an idea.

33

"I know a swell game we could play with the snowman," he said to himself. "I'm going to take him into the hall and fix everything up. Then, when they're through playing Going to Jerusalem, I'll tell everybody about it."

The snowman was too heavy for Norman to lift, but he found that by tilting it over he could drag it into the house. He did this, and stood the white figure up near a window seat in the hall. Then he went back to the living room.

The other children were still playing Going to Jerusalem, so Norman had to wait a few minutes. Before he had a chance to tell anyone his idea for a new game, Mrs. Camp got up from the piano stool and said:

"Now, I have a special guessing game planned. I'll play a record of various kinds of sounds. You must guess what they are."

As the children listened they found it was easy at first to identify a cat, a dog, and an automobile horn. But as the record kept on playing, it became harder and harder for them to guess the sounds. Mrs. Camp had to play parts of the record over and over again.

"Now this is the last time for these two," she said finally.

34

Suddenly Grace Winters called out, "Oh, I know that sound. That's birds' wings! I heard it last summer when a little robin flew into our house."

"Good for you!" said Mrs. Camp. "Let's see if anyone can guess the last one on the record."

The children sat very quiet as the sound was played once more. Suddenly Honey Bunch clapped her hands.

"It's a wagon going over the snow!" she exclaimed.

"That's right!" smiled Ida's mother.

"I guess I knew it 'cause my mind's on going up North," said Honey Bunch. She often heard Mrs. Miller say her mind was on something when she seemed to be thinking real hard.

Norman had been so interested in trying to guess the strange sounds that for a while he had forgotten all about the snowman in the hall. Just as he was ready to suggest his new game, Ida's mother announced that the children were to go into the dining room at once and have ice cream. So he did not say anything.

Honey Bunch, who was the guest of honor, went in first. There was a lovely surprise for her. At her place was a little present from Ida.

It was a pair of snow-white moccasins with soft fur trimming.

"Oh!" cried Honey Bunch, holding them up so the fur could touch her cheek. "I love them! Thank you, Ida!"

The other children asked Honey Bunch to tell them about her trip, so she told about Christina and Snowtop Inn, and the entertainment there for children.

"Oh, you're going to have a wonderful time!" said Dorothy Finch. "I wish I were going with you!"

"So do I!" "So do I!" cried out all the other children.

Honey Bunch promised to tell her friends about her first winter at Snowtop as soon as she got back. In a few minutes she looked outdoors and was surprised to see that it was dark. She knew that it was time for her to leave. She told Mrs. Camp and Ida what fun she had had, and said she must go home. She was the first of the guests to start for the stairs to get her coat and hat.

As the little girl came into the hall, she gasped in astonishment. Before her stood the snowman, but he was no longer a complete snowman.

A great deal of him had melted all over the floor.

"Oh! Oh!" she cried out.

"What's the matter?" asked Ida, who was just behind her.

"There's a flood in your hall!" cried out Honey Bunch.

CHAPTER IV

ON THE TRAIN

At Honey Bunch's words Mrs. Camp ran forward. When she saw the water in the hall, she gasped.

"Oh, my goodness!" she cried. "Who brought in the snowman?"

Suddenly Norman Clark realized what had happened. He felt dreadfully ashamed.

"I—I did," he stammered.

Mrs. Camp got busy at once. She opened the front door, slid the snowman across the hall, and pushed him outside. She called to Ida to run to the kitchen and bring a broom.

"Can I do anything?" Honey Bunch asked her.

"Yes," said Mrs. Camp. "Run upstairs and bring some Turkish towels from the closet. Put them on the floor in the doorway to the living room. I don't want the rug in there to get wet."

Honey Bunch ran to the second floor as fast as she could. She knew where the linen closet was

38

and quickly grabbed up a pile of Turkish towels. Then she hurried downstairs and piled them into the doorway of the living room. The water already was beginning to run across the sill.

Ida returned with the broom, and Mrs. Camp began to sweep the water from the hall onto the front porch.

Norman did not know what to do. He was so frightened and ashamed he could think of nothing to say. He decided that perhaps the best thing he could do was to go home quietly. So he went upstairs and got his coat and hat.

But by the time Norman came downstairs again, he decided not to go without saying something to Mrs. Camp. Again, he repeated that he was very sorry. He also said he had had a very good time at the party and would never do such a naughty thing again.

In the meantime Honey Bunch was helping Ida take things out of the window seat box. Ida kept many of her toys there and some of them were soaked with water which had run inside. They would have to be dried out. A couple of her playthings were ruined.

"I'm never going to ask Norman to my house again," Ida declared, looking mournfully at a big red kite which she never could fly again.

Honey Bunch was afraid Ida meant what she said. She knew that Norman had not intended to cause so much trouble, and she decided then and there she would have to do something about it. After dinner when Norman came over to her house to ask her what he could do to make up for his mistake, she promptly replied:

"You can give Ida your kite."

Norman was shocked. He had a very beautiful kite which he prized highly. He felt as if he would rather part with almost any other toy than this one. But Honey Bunch was very insistent.

"You ruined Ida's kite and some of her other things too. Besides, you made a lot of work for Mrs. Camp."

"Oh, all right," Norman said at last. "I'll do it."

He kept his word, and the next morning left his fine kite at Ida's home. Honey Bunch did not know about this until later, because her cousin Stub arrived early that day. The two little girls were having a lot of fun talking about the trip to Snowtop.

"My mother made me bring so many warm

40

clothes my suitcase is ready to burst," announced Stub, giggling. "Why are you looking at me so funny, Honey Bunch?" she asked.

"Because you're not my size any more," her cousin replied. "Stub, you must have been eating an awful lot on your farm lately."

It was true that Stub had taken on a good bit of weight since Honey Bunch had seen her last. The new snowsuit which Mrs. Morton had bought for Stub would not fit her now. Honey Bunch showed it to her.

"I guess we'll have to get another one," she said.

Mrs. Morton took both little girls to the Kiddie Shop. Stub tried on several snowsuits before they found a waterproof one which was the right size. It was bright red.

"We can't be twins now," said Honey Bunch, "because mine's blue." Then she added, "Oh, here comes Christina!"

Little Christina Vasa had seen Honey Bunch and her mother from across the store. Now she walked over to speak to them. She was glad to meet Stub, and told them she could hardly wait for them to visit Snowtop.

"When you come to my house," she said, "I'll

show you my dolls. Maybe you've never seen any like them."

"Why, are they different?" Stub wanted to know.

"They're from Sweden and they are dressed in all kinds of costumes. There aren't any like them in this store."

She took Honey Bunch and Stub over to the doll counter, and they looked at every doll in the store. Honey Bunch did not say so, but she thought her own dolls at home were prettier than any she saw here.

"Wouldn't you like to go home with us and see *my* dolls?" she asked Christina. "I have some special ones, too."

"Have you still got the Oriental one the lady at the Big Fair gave you?" Stub asked her cousin.

"Oh, yes," said Honey Bunch. "She's one of my fav'rite dolls."

The little girl told Christina about the time she and Stub had visited the Big Fair, and what fun they had had, and how Stub had become lost.

"It was kind of scary," giggled Stub. "I don't ever want to be lost that way again."

Christina said she would like to go to Honey

42

Bunch's house if Mrs. Harden would let her.

"She's the lady my father and I are staying with," Christina explained.

"Does she own that nice dog Trix?" Honey Bunch asked her. "He pulls sleds and carries packages," she explained to her cousin.

"I want to see him," said Stub.

"He's next door at the butcher shop with Mrs. Harden," Christina told her. "She told me to wait here for her."

Honey Bunch and Stub wished Mrs. Harden would hurry. Pretty soon they saw her and the lovely collie dog coming out of the store. He was carrying the handle of a basket in his mouth. In the basket were several packages.

"Oh, isn't he just wonderful!" cried Honey Bunch.

When Trix walked into the Kiddie Shop, she patted him. Stub patted him too. Then suddenly Stub ran to the toy counter. Without thinking, she picked up a white woolly toy dog and wound up the little machine inside of it. Then Stub set the toy dog on the floor, and he walked along saying "Bowwow!"

At once Trix dropped his basket and bounded over to the toy. Of course, he knew it was not

43

real, but he probably thought the little dog was making fun of him with his barking. He could not have this!

Before anyone could stop him, Trix picked up the toy in his teeth and shook it just as hard as he could. Mrs. Harden hurried over and tried to get it away from him. But the dog only ran off, tossing the woolly toy from side to side.

"He'll ruin it!" cried the salesgirl who had sold Mrs. Morton the snowsuits.

Trix was having a very good time. He would set the white dog down, but as soon as anyone would come near him, he would pick it up again and off he would go!

The children ran after him, but this only made him think it was a game.

"Trix! Drop that!" Mrs. Harden cried finally in a very stern voice.

Trix knew the fun was over. He dropped the white dog, ran back to his basket and picked it up. He was ready for work again.

The toy was not ruined, but it was dirty and wet. It could not be offered for sale again. Stub said she would pay for it from some money her daddy had given her, but Mrs. Harden declared this was not necessary.

"I'll buy the dog for Trix," she said. "I don't know what made him do such a thing. He knows better."

Honey Bunch asked Mrs. Harden if Christina could go home with her to play. When she said "yes," the three little girls hurried up the street ahead of Mrs. Morton.

Christina stayed at Honey Bunch's house longer than she expected to. She was delighted with the little girl's toys, and they played for several hours with them. Kindly Mrs. Miller served luncheon for the three children in the playroom, where there was a small table and dishes.

"Everything at your house is different from mine," said Christina. "And your toys are too. But you'll like mine. When you visit me, I'm going to give you one of my dolls, Honey Bunch."

She would have offered one to Stub also, but Stub had announced while they were eating that she really did not care very much for dolls. She liked other toys better, especially boys' toys.

At four o'clock Mrs. Harden came to get Christina, saying her daddy wanted her to pack to go home.

"We're going on a sleeping train tonight," Christina said. "It's lots of fun."

Honey Bunch and Stub hoped that they would go to Snowtop this way too. Sleeping on a train could be very exciting!

Not long after Christina had gone, Mr. Morton came home. At once the children asked him whether he had made arrangements for them to go to Snowtop Inn on a sleeping train.

"Yes, I have," he answered, "but I'm disappointed with our reservations. I had hoped we might have a couple of rooms to ourselves, but all I could get were three lower berths."

He explained that in a sleeper there were two rows of beds, one above the other. Each bed, which was called a berth, had a curtain in front of it so no one could see the people sleeping. The bottom berths were called "lowers," and those which were reached by climbing a ladder were called "uppers."

"When are we going, Daddy?" his small daughter asked.

"Tomorrow night, dear," he replied.

The next day Honey Bunch and Stub were very busy packing their suitcases. Mother and Mrs. Miller helped them, and by the time Mr.

46

Morton came home the little girls were ready to leave.

"Will we eat on the train?" Stub wanted to know.

"No, dear," Mrs. Morton spoke up. "We'll have an early dinner here and then get on the sleeper at eight o'clock."

It was decided that it would be best not to open the main pieces of baggage on the train, so the night clothes of the four Mortons were put into one small bag. As Stub took her pajamas out of her suitcase, she asked what time they would have to get up in the morning. She was told at half past six.

"We have to get off the train at seven," said Mrs. Morton, "so that will give us half an hour to dress."

Mrs. Miller had prepared a delicious dinner, but Honey Bunch and Stub were so excited about going away they could hardly eat. At last it was half past seven, and a taxi driver drew up in front of the Morton home and tooted his horn.

"Everyone ready?" called Daddy.

Honey Bunch ran off to bid one last good-bye to Mrs. Miller, saying she hoped the woman would not work so hard that she would be on her

47

"last legs" by the time the little girl got home.

The taxicab brought them to the station in plenty of time. Honey Bunch and Stub Morton watched in awe as the big train roared into the station. Then they climbed aboard. The friendly porter was making up the beds, and the little girls followed him from seat to seat, watching the man as he pulled down one berth after another from the ceiling.

Since it was bedtime for the little girls, they could not stay up to see him finish his work. Mrs. Morton took the overnight bag into the dressing room at the end of the car, and there the children put on their pajamas. Honey Bunch had brought her new little snow-white moccasins and put them on for the first time.

"Please be very quiet after you get into bed," said Mrs. Morton. "No talking and no giggling. We have to get up very early, and you'll need all the sleep you can get."

It was hard for the little cousins to obey. They did whisper for a few minutes, but the gentle jouncing of the train as it sped through the night soon rocked them to sleep.

It seemed like a long time after she had fallen asleep that Honey Bunch woke up. Someone was pushing her. At first she did not know where she was. It was very dark and her bed did not stay still on the floor. Suddenly she heard a train whistle and then she remembered she was on the sleeper.

"Honey Bunch, are you awake?" asked her cousin, who lay beside her.

"Yes, Stub. What do you want?"

Stub said she had to have a drink of water. She had been awake a long time and was very thirsty. She was sure she could not stand it another minute, and wanted Honey Bunch to go to the end of the train with her for some ice water.

"I don't think Mother would like us to get up," said Honey Bunch. It was very still in the train, and she knew everyone had gone to bed.

"I can't help it. I'm so thirsty I can't sleep," Stub insisted. "We'll only be a minute."

Finally, feeling sorry for her cousin, Honey Bunch was persuaded to go. She and Stub put on their bathrobes and slippers; then Honey Bunch pushed aside the curtains and the two little girls stepped into the aisle.

On tiptoe they went to the dressing room. Stub had three cups of water. Honey Bunch had not thought she was thirsty, but when she saw Stub drinking she too had some water.

"We'd better go back now," she told Stub, and opened the door.

She led the way down the aisle. Suddenly she stopped and turned around, almost bumping into Stub.

"What's the matter?" whispered her cousin.

"I don't know where our bed is," said Honey Bunch.

Stub did not know either. The two little girls walked up and down the aisle several times. They did not have the least notion where their berth was.

Honey Bunch had an idea. She would ask the nice porter. But though she went to each end of the sleeper she could not find him.

"Now what are we going to do?" asked Stub. "We can't stand up in the train all night."

CHAPTER V

SNOWTOP INN

THE train porter, coming back from the dining car where he had had his midnight supper, opened the door of the sleeping car. There, against the wall, were two scared little girls.

"Mah goodness," he said in surprise, "what in de world you-all doin' here?"

"We're lost from our beds," Honey Bunch answered.

"I'll fix dat up right away," smiled the big man. He took a piece of paper from his pocket and looked at it. "You're in Lower Seven," he told them.

"How can you tell?" Stub asked him. "We didn't give you our names."

The porter smiled. "I have my own special way of knowing," he said. "Lots of people get lost on trains, so I write things down. Here it says, 'Upper Six, red-haired man; Lower Five, stout lady; and Lower Seven, two little girls.'"

Honey Bunch and Stub giggled, then remembered they must be quiet. They followed the porter to their berth and climbed in. It seemed to Honey Bunch as if she had hardly gone to sleep when she was awakened again.

But this time it was not by her cousin. Stub was sound asleep, but in a moment she too woke up. Somewhere near them was a buzzing sound. As they listened, it turned into a ringing noise. Though muffled, the noise was loud enough to wake everyone up.

"What do you s'pose it is?" Honey Bunch asked her cousin. "It's right under us."

"I—I guess it's my alarm clock," Stub replied.

She said this so loud Mrs. Morton in the next berth heard her. She came at once and opened the curtains to the little girls' berth.

"Where is the clock?" she asked quickly.

"In my suitcase."

Mrs. Morton drew Stub's bag from beneath the berth and tried to open it. Finding it locked, she asked for the key. Stub looked through her little purse but the key was not there.

"Please hurry, Stub!" said Mrs. Morton. "We'll wake everybody up!"

Stub did not know what to do. People began

to peer out between their curtains and complain about the noise.

"Maybe the key's in your coat pocket," suggested Honey Bunch.

Stub stood up and tried to feel in the pockets of her coat which was hanging on a hook. But the train made it sway back and forth, and she could not get her hand inside. Finally Honey Bunch helped her.

The key was not there, and the alarm on the clock was still ringing!

"Stub, can't you find the key?" her aunt asked.

The poor little girl burst into tears. More and more people were calling out to stop the clock. The porter had come down the aisle by this time, and said he had better break the bag open and turn off the alarm.

Just then the clock stopped ringing. Honey Bunch sighed, and said she guessed it had worn itself out. Mrs. Morton remarked that she felt she was worn out too. She asked Stub what time the alarm had been set for, and the little girl answered that she had tried to fix it for six-thirty.

"That's the time you said we have to get up. But I must have put it at the wrong number."

"You surely did," said Mrs. Morton, glanc-

53

ing at her wrist watch. "It's only half past four. Now go to sleep and don't worry about getting up. I'll call you when it's time."

Everyone in the sleeper settled down once more. At half past six, Mr. and Mrs. Morton and the children got up and dressed quickly. Presently the train pulled into a station and they got off. Mr. Morton counted the suitcases to be sure none of them were left on the train. The nice porter said "good-bye" to the little girls, and hoped they would have a good time at Snowtop. It was not until the train was out of sight that Stub gave a little squeal.

"Oh!" she said. "I left my socks on the train!"

"Goodness," said her Aunt Edith, "I wonder if we left anything else."

Honey Bunch suddenly looked upset. "I'm afraid I left my gloves on the train," she said.

Mrs. Morton told her daughter to put her hands in her pockets to keep them warm. It was very cold, and they had a long drive ahead of them. As the little girls looked around, it seemed to them as if they could see nothing but mountains and mountains of snow.

At this moment they heard sleigh bells, and

down the road came a large sleigh and a team of horses. The driver was bundled up so that only a small portion of his face showed. He wore a reddish-brown snowsuit and a cap which covered his entire head except his eyes and nose and mouth. The tip of his nose was bright red. His blue eyes twinkled, and when he saw the Morton family he gave them a big smile.

The jolly man jumped out and put the suitcases in the rear of the sleigh. Then he helped Mrs. Morton into the back seat.

"How about the two little ladies sitting up front with me?" he asked, smiling at Honey Bunch and Stub.

They thought it would be fun to watch him drive so they climbed in. Mr. Morton seated himself beside his wife. The driver bundled up his passengers with furry robes, and hopping aboard said:

"Giddap!"

Off the horses trotted. Mr. and Mrs. Morton remarked about the lovely countryside, but Honey Bunch was not looking at the scenery. She could not keep her eyes off the man next to her. Finally she had to tell him what was on her mind.

55

"You look just like Santa Claus," she said.

The driver laughed, and said he'd certainly like to be Santa Claus. But since he couldn't, maybe he could be something like him.

"You know, my name is Ross," he told her. "Perhaps you'd like to call me Santa Ross."

Honey Bunch took her hands from her pockets and clapped them in delight.

"That will be wonderful!" she said. "All the time I'm at Snowtop I can make believe you're Santa Claus. He's supposed to live way, way up North and you do too. There's lots and lots of snow at his home, and there is at yours, too." She looked up at him and said sweetly, "Yes, I'm going to call you Santa Ross."

Stub thought this was a very good idea, and decided she too would call the man by this name. As they drove along, the children told him the funny things which had happened on the sleeper and he laughed heartily.

It seemed to Honey Bunch they never would stop going uphill. After a while she asked Santa Ross if they weren't on top of the world. He said he guessed they just about were, and that it was quite the loveliest place in all the world to live.

"You mean in the summertime too?" Honey Bunch wanted to know.

The driver nodded, but said he liked it best of all in the wintertime. As they rounded a sharp curve, he stopped the horses for a moment and pointed ahead.

"There's Snowtop Inn," he announced.

At first the Mortons could not make out the building. All they could see were hills and hills of white snow. But a few minutes later they knew why they could not see the hotel. Snowtop Inn was painted white and its roof was covered with glistening snow.

"Oh!" gasped Honey Bunch. "It's just like a giant's snowhouse!"

She and Stub were a little worried. They had never heard of a snowhouse which was really warm inside. One always had to be bundled up when inside one, and they did not think it would be very nice to live at Snowtop Inn with their heavy clothes on all the time. They were surprised when Santa Ross seemed to read their thoughts.

"Snowtop Inn is cozy and warm inside, even though it looks cold on the outside," he said. "I'm sure you'll like it here."

He pulled up to the big front door of the Inn, and a boy came out to help him carry the bags. Honey Bunch jumped out by herself and caught up with her daddy, who was just going inside. When she walked into the big lobby of the hotel, the little girl gasped.

"Oh, Daddy, isn't this just the nicest place you ever saw!" she exclaimed.

At one end of the room was the biggest fireplace Honey Bunch had ever seen, and the biggest fire she had ever seen was burning in it. Some of the logs were six feet long.

On the floor were heavy rugs, and comfortable furniture was placed attractively around the room. Beautiful bouquets of flowers stood on the tables. In a sunny window several canary birds were singing merrily in their cages.

Daddy Morton walked up to the hotel desk and signed the register. The clerk said he was glad they had arrived safely and trusted they would enjoy their stay at Snowtop. Honey Bunch was quite sure they would!

The clerk handed two keys to a bellboy, saying the Mortons' rooms were on the third floor. They went up in an elevator and the boy led them to the end of the hall. After Mrs. Morton

58

had looked over the two adjoining rooms, she decided that she and Daddy would take the larger one since they had more bags. Honey Bunch had never thought about it before, but of course Mother's dresses took up more room in a suitcase than hers did.

"That's why Mother needed two bags and I have only one," she told herself. Aloud she said, "Are we going to unpack right away?"

Daddy said breakfast was being served and he was very hungry. He wanted to eat before they did any unpacking.

"We may as well eat," said Mrs. Morton, "because we have to find someone to unlock Stub's bag before we can take out her clothes. But first we'll wash our hands and comb our hair."

Honey Bunch had run to the window to look outside. She wanted to see exactly what the top of the world looked like. The little girl decided it was a beautiful sight. Not far from the Inn were two lakes, a big one and a little one. In the distance was a hill for toboggans and skiers.

"Come, dear," said her father, "or they may eat up all the food downstairs, and then what would we do?"

Honey Bunch laughed, and scampered off to

wash her face and hands. She had not yet learned to comb her curls very well alone, so Mother had to help her do this.

Stub almost kept them from getting down to the dining room in time for breakfast. She turned on the faucet in the basin too hard, and the water splashed up on her dress. But Mrs. Morton stood her in front of a register in the wall, and the heat dried the dress quickly.

"I wonder how many children are at Snowtop," said Honey Bunch as they went down in the elevator.

The young man who ran it told her there were about thirty boys and girls, and that they had lots of fun.

"You'll enjoy eating in the children's dining room," he told them. "But no one is in it now. Only the early risers eat there. The boys and girls who come down late have breakfast with their parents in the main dining room."

"We were early risers three times today," said Honey Bunch. "But two of the times we went back to bed."

"And it was a long drive to the hotel," Stub told him.

When the Mortons reached the main dining

room, they were shown to a table near a window where they could look out and see the people who already were at play. Their waitress was named Jenny, and Honey Bunch liked her very much. She reminded her of Mrs. Miller's niece who sometimes came to work at the Mortons' home in Barham.

"What would you like for breakfast?" she asked sweetly. "The oatmeal is very good. Maybe you'd enjoy some Snowtop honey and some cream on it?"

Honey Bunch and Stub thought they would like this, and they also asked for fruit and cocoa. Daddy decided on sausage and pancakes, and Mother teased him about eating so much.

"But I don't blame you," she said. "The food is delicious."

Just as they finished eating, a very pretty young woman came to their table. She introduced herself as Miss Dorothy Allen, and said she was the children's hostess. Honey Bunch and Stub were not sure what she meant, and Mother explained that she took care of all the entertainment for the boys and girls who were staying at the Inn.

"I thought you would like to meet the rest of

our young guests," she said, smiling at the little girls.

"You mean all thirty of them?" Stub asked.

Miss Allen laughed and said:

"Yes, all thirty of them. Every morning we meet in the playroom to do our exercises and dance. Then I tell everyone about the plans for the day. We're ready to start now. Wouldn't you like to come along?"

CHAPTER VI

A TROUBLESOME PLAYMATE

THE children's playroom was large and had every kind of indoor toy one could think of. There were even slides and swings which are usually found only outdoors.

When Honey Bunch and Stub walked in with Miss Allen, many boys and girls were already there. The hostess took the two cousins around to meet the children, who all seemed to be very friendly. Honey Bunch was sure she was going to enjoy playing with them.

In a few moments an eight-year-old boy ran up to Miss Allen. He called her Aunt Dorothy, and the woman introduced him as her nephew Billy. She said he was staying at the Inn for a short time.

"I live in New York," he told the cousins. "Where do you live?"

Honey Bunch explained that she came from Barham and that Stub lived on a farm. Miss Allen asked the little girls if they liked to dance, and they both answered, yes, they did very much.

After Miss Allen had walked away, Stub told Billy that her cousin was a very good dancer. He smiled at Honey Bunch.

"When we have the dancing lesson this morning, I'll come and get you for a partner," he said.

Honey Bunch thought Billy Allen was a very nice boy to ask her to be his partner. She did not notice that another girl had joined them and overheard the conversation. Her name was Susan Jane Black, and she always wanted Billy to play with her and no one else. Now she did not like it because he had asked Honey Bunch to dance with him.

When Billy walked away, she said to Honey Bunch, "You needn't think you can come here and take my friends away from me!"

Honey Bunch was so surprised she opened her eyes wide. "I'm not trying to take your friends away," she denied.

Susan Jane turned and spoke to some of the other children. She laughed rather loudly and said, "Let's give the new girls our club test."

"What's that?" asked Stub.

"We have our own club here," Susan Jane explained. "It's called the Children's Club. You have to answer a special question before you can join. If you don't know the answer, you can't play with the rest of us."

Honey Bunch and Stub were worried. Susan Jane spoke as if she might be the president of the club. They hoped they would know the answer to whatever she was going to ask them.

"What do you skate on?" Susan Jane asked.

"Ice, of course," Stub replied. "That's easy."

"What do you think, Honey Bunch?" Susan Jane asked.

Honey Bunch gave the same answer as her cousin, but to her surprise Susan Jane told them they were wrong. She said neither of them could join the Children's Club and began to laugh loudly at their failure.

Miss Allen, who heard her, wondered what was going on. Now she came over, and Susan Jane told her what she had asked the new children.

"I'm sorry you didn't know the answer," Miss Allen said kindly to Honey Bunch and Stub. "But that makes no difference about your joining the Children's Club. As a matter of fact, no one has ever guessed the right answer—not even Susan Jane."

Then she told Honey Bunch and Stub that the right answer is water. Ice is not slippery, and therefore one could not skate on it. It would be like trying to skate on a smooth stone.

"What is slippery is the water, which is made by your skates going over the ice and melting it," the young woman explained. "You can hardly see the water, and when the weather is very cold, it freezes right back into ice. But really you are skating on water," she smiled at Honey Bunch and Stub.

Susan Jane was very angry since she had not had her own way, and walked off toward the other side of the room. At this moment Miss Allen clapped her hands loudly and the children formed into two lines. The hostess found places for Honey Bunch and Stub, and then called out the exercises. The two cousins knew some of the exercises, but several of them were new. They had fun trying to imitate the rest of the children.

Honey Bunch and Stub had such a good time, they forgot all about their trouble with Susan Jane. But as soon as Miss Allen announced the dancing, Susan Jane rushed up to Billy and pulled him onto the floor. The boy did not

know what to do. He already had asked Honey
Bunch, but she smiled to let him know she did
not mind.

She accepted the invitation of a little boy
named Sammy Simms. They had a very good
time together. Billy, watching her, knew at
once that she was a better dancer than Susan
Jane.

When the program was over, Honey Bunch
and Stub hurried upstairs to their room. Daddy
had gone off to find someone to open Stub's suitcase. Mother had hung up all her own clothes
and Daddy's, and now she was putting Honey
Bunch's dresses in the closet. Presently Mr.
Morton returned. With him was Santa Ross.

"Are you having a good time?" the sleigh
driver asked, his eyes twinkling.

"Oh, we've been having lots of fun," said
Honey Bunch, "and we found out what you
skate on."

Santa Ross said he knew the right answer, but
she should ask her father the riddle. Even Mr.
Morton said "Ice," and that made Honey Bunch
feel better about her own mistake.

"You took off your Santa Claus clothes," she
said to Santa Ross.

The man explained laughingly that he saved those clothes for the times he went to meet little girls at the station. Now he had on overalls, and from one of his pockets he pulled out the biggest bunch of keys Honey Bunch had ever seen. Santa Ross knelt down on the floor and tried the keys on Stub's suitcase. At last he found one which fitted, and they heard the lock click.

"Oh, thank you, thank you," said Stub. "Now I can set my alarm clock to the right getting-up time."

In the meantime Honey Bunch had been wondering about something. She asked Santa Ross if he had lived at Snowtop all his life. When she learned he had been there since he was a little boy, she inquired if he knew the Vasas.

"I mean, the ones who have a daughter named Christina and a son Axel," she explained.

"Oh, yes, I know them very well," the man replied. "Very fine people. Mr. Vasa makes the most beautiful jewelry I have ever seen."

"He showed some of it to us," said Honey Bunch.

"Oh, then you have met the family?" asked Santa Ross.

Honey Bunch told him that she knew only Christina and her father, but hoped to meet Mrs. Vasa and Axel soon.

"It's too bad they had to have so much trouble," said Santa Ross.

"Trouble?" Honey Bunch repeated. "Did they have a lot of trouble?"

Santa Ross told the Mortons that Mr. Vasa had lost a great deal of money, or at least a great deal of jewelry which he intended to sell.

"He gave it to a messenger, a local boy, who drove to the station with it. Then he was to take the train to New York to deliver the package. But somehow the jewelry disappeared. The boy said he lost it, but some of the folks around here think he stole it."

"How dreadful!" said Honey Bunch. "And what became of the boy?"

Santa Ross said that he had gone away, and the boxes of jewelry had never been found. After the sleigh driver left the room, Honey Bunch ran up to her daddy, climbed on his lap, and said:

"Do you suppose that boy really did take that jewelry? If he did, maybe he's one of those bad men who's making some like it now."

Daddy looked down at his small daughter. "You're a very wise little girl," he said, "and you may be right. The cheap pins which look like Mr. Vasa's good ones are perhaps being made by that very messenger. I'll look into the matter."

During this conversation Stub had become a little bored. She had not heard the story about the jewelry, and was more interested in watching the chambermaids who were working in the various rooms. She ran down the hall to see what they were doing. Stub noticed that each time they brought soiled linen from a room, they opened a small door in the hall and almost instantly the sheets, pillowcases and towels disappeared.

"Where do they go to?" she asked one of the chambermaids whose name was Nellie.

"Down to the laundry," the maid answered.

Stub wanted to know how they got there, and Nellie explained that they went down a long chute.

"Is it a clothes toboggan slide?" Stub asked.

"Well, you might call it that," Nellie laughed. "Anyway, the linen slides from here all the way down to the cellar."

70

The idea fascinated Stub. She watched the chambermaids until they finished their work and left the third floor.

"Maybe this could be a little girl's slide too," she said to herself.

Without thinking of what might happen to her, Stub Morton opened the door to the clothes chute, climbed up, and crawled inside.

CHAPTER VII

CHUTE-THE-CHUTES

BACK in the children's bedroom fifteen minutes went by before the Mortons missed Stub. Honey Bunch had been talking about the Vasas and the lost jewelry and Mrs. Morton was unpacking Stub's suitcase.

"Where is Stub?" she asked.

Honey Bunch jumped down from her daddy's lap and looked out in the hall. She did not see her cousin.

"Prob'ly Stub went downstairs," she told her mother. "I'll find her."

But Stub was not on the first floor of the hotel. Honey Bunch looked all over the lobby, in the children's playroom, and in all the rooms where the grownups played games. She asked the clerk at the desk, the men who ran the elevators, and the lady at the newspaper stand. None of them had seen Stub.

"Oh, dear," said Honey Bunch. "I wonder where she is."

Honey Bunch felt sure her cousin was not out-doors, because it was too cold to stay out very long without a coat. And she knew Stub's coat and snowsuit were upstairs.

She went back to the room and told her parents that Stub was nowhere around. Mr. and Mrs. Morton became rather concerned and went off to look for their little niece. Honey Bunch, left alone, sat down in a chair to think.

"When Norman and I had a mystery to solve one time," she said to herself, "how did we do it? Oh, I remember. We spoke to the last person who saw the lost one. Now, who saw Stub last?"

After thinking very hard for several minutes, Honey Bunch remembered seeing the chamber-maids in the hall as she and Stub had come up-stairs from the children's playroom. Perhaps Stub went with one of them to watch her work.

Honey Bunch found a back stairway and went down to the second floor. The maids were at work there. Going up to the one called Nellie, she asked the woman if she had seen her cousin.

"Well, I'm not sure," said the chambermaid. "What does your cousin look like?"

Honey Bunch said Stub was a little fatter than she was, and that she usually ran instead of walking. She often stubbed her toe and fell down. Nellie laughed at the description, and said she guessed it must have been Stub who was talking to her in the hall upstairs.

"She's lost," said Honey Bunch. "Did she say anything to help us find her?"

"Oh, your cousin is lost?" Nellie said. "That's too bad."

"Yes," said Honey Bunch, "and I'm trying to be a detective and find her. Were you the last person who saw her? Would you mind putting on your thinking cap and telling me?"

The chambermaid smiled at Honey Bunch's expression. She thought the little girl sounded very old-fashioned for one so young. Of course she did not know that Honey Bunch had heard Mrs. Miller say this very thing many times at her home in Barham. It was one of the laundress' favorite expressions.

The chambermaid said she would put on her thinking cap. Suddenly an idea came to her.

"Do you suppose," she said, "do you suppose— Oh, my goodness!"

Honey Bunch wondered what the maid was

74

trying to say. She became rather frightened as a worried look came over Nellie's face.

"Maybe—maybe your cousin went down the clothes chute!" she exclaimed.

Honey Bunch did not understand what Nellie meant. Quickly the woman told her. Then, taking Honey Bunch by the hand, she whisked her down the back stairway to the cellar. Almost running across the floor, she went straight to a door and opened it. Out tumbled dozens and dozens of sheets, pillowcases and towels. And with them came Stub Morton!

Honey Bunch stared at her small cousin. Nellie picked up Stub and asked her if she was all right. The little girl said she was not hurt in the least, but she certainly was glad to be out of the clothes toboggan slide. It was very dark and hot in there. Also, she had been kept very busy pulling sheets and pillowcases off her head as they had been thrown down on top of her.

Now that Honey Bunch's fright was over, she began to laugh. Nellie laughed too, and after a while Stub joined in.

"We'd better go upstairs," said Honey Bunch. "Mother and Daddy are worried about you, Stub."

It was a good thing the little girls did go upstairs at once, because Mr. and Mrs. Morton were becoming alarmed. Not only had Stub disappeared, but their own little girl was gone as well. Stub promised not to wander off again.

"I think we'll go outdoors now," said Mrs. Morton. "Put on your snowsuits, children, and we'll take a walk."

Daddy Morton had been looking around outside Snowtop Inn after breakfast, so he knew exactly where to take his wife and the little girls to show them the sights. Nearly all the visitors at the hotel were outdoors enjoying the lovely sunny day. Many of them had gone off to the ski run, others were sleigh riding, and a number of them were on the big pond skating.

"Oh, look at that little girl!" cried Honey Bunch, as they came to the pond. "See what she can do!"

On the ice were a tall man and a little girl about the age of Honey Bunch and Stub. She was doing all the fancy skating steps the man did, and when some music was played over a loud speaker, they danced very prettily together.

"Who is she, Daddy?" Honey Bunch asked.

"I understand she's the man's daughter," Mr.

Morton replied, "and he is the skating instructor here."

"Oh, he must be Rudy!" Honey Bunch cried. "Mr. Vasa told us about him. What's his daughter's name?"

"I don't know," Daddy Morton replied. "Let's go speak to them."

The little girl's name was Mitzi. She was very dainty and soft spoken, and said she had been skating since she was two years old.

"Maybe you'd like to see my very first skates," she said to Honey Bunch and Stub. "They're up at the clubhouse."

"Oh, we'd love to!" they said.

Mitzi took off her skates and handed them to her father. He said he would take care of them till she came back from the clubhouse.

Her first skates were so tiny that Honey Bunch and Stub wondered how anyone could have skated on them. Pinned on the wall near them were several ribbons with gold letters on them. Some of the ribbons were blue and some were red.

"What are these?" Stub wanted to know.

Mitzi laughed. "Oh, they are prizes I won in exhibitions. I skate lots of places."

77

"Why are they different colors?" Stub asked.

Mitzi explained that the blue ribbon was for first prize, red was for second, and if there was a third, it was always white. Honey Bunch and Stub thought it was wonderful that Mitzi had received so many prizes.

They asked her if she skated with her father in exhibitions. The little girl said not always. She liked it best when he was her partner, but sometimes she had to skate alone.

"Did you bring your skates?" Mitzi asked them.

Honey Bunch and Stub said they had not, and that they did not skate very well anyway. When she heard this, Mitzi said she owned several pairs of skates, and was sure hers would fit the girls. She insisted they borrow them and come out on the ice with her sometime. The two little cousins thanked Mitzi, and then said they must go back to Mr. and Mrs. Morton.

"We have to see the rest of Snowtop," Honey Bunch told the little skating champion.

"You must take a ride with the Eskimo dogs," Mitzi advised. "It's lots of fun!"

This was exactly what Honey Bunch and Stub did. Daddy Morton already had arranged for a little trip. He and his small daughter would ride on one of the sleds, and Mrs. Morton and Stub would go on the other.

The sleds were drawn by several big dogs. They were harnessed in pairs, and at the head of each team was a single dog. He was the leader. The driver stood at the back of the sled behind his passengers.

"Are Eskimo dogs friendly?" Stub asked. She thought they looked like pictures of wolves she had seen.

"They won't hurt you," the driver replied. "But they're strictly outdoor dogs. Not lap dogs."

Honey Bunch and Stub giggled to think what it would be like to hold one of the big animals on their laps. They went over to stroke two of the dogs.

"These dogs have another name," said the man. "It's huskies."

Stub thought she liked the word Eskimo better, because it made her think of the place the dogs came from. She asked what they ate.

"Down here they eat meat and dog crackers, but the Eskimos feed them dried fish," the driver said. "The dogs gobble up the fish and

79

then swallow chunks of snow for a drink!"

Honey Bunch asked how the dogs could keep warm inside if they ate snow, and the man replied he guessed it was because they exercised so hard. He said that if everyone were ready, they would push off on the sleds. He teasingly asked Honey Bunch if she knew what to say to make the dogs start.

"Mush!" she answered unexpectedly.

The huskies started off at once. Honey Bunch felt very proud to have remembered the right word.

"Christina told it to me," she explained to her daddy.

The dogs ran very fast—first across an open space, then through a lovely, sweet-smelling pine woods. Finally they came to a hill. It was not very steep and the dogs did not seem to mind the climb.

When they reached the top of the hill the drivers stopped the sleds. Honey Bunch looked about in surprise. This side of the hill was very long and steep. In fact, it was about a mile to the bottom. The toboggan slide was located here, and Honey Bunch watched the long sleds whiz down the slope.

"May we go on one, Daddy?" she asked excitedly.

Her father smiled at her. "Would you really like to? And you wouldn't be frightened? You know the sleds go like the wind."

Honey Bunch looked up at him. "I'd never be frightened if you were with me," she said.

Mr. Morton squeezed his small daughter's hand. Then he asked Mother and Stub if they would like to go along. Mrs. Morton said she guessed not, and Stub, after a moment's thought, decided she had had enough tobogganing for one morning. Her swift race down the clothes-chute had made her lose interest in this kind of sport.

"Stub and I will ride home with the Eskimo dogs," Mrs. Morton decided. "We'll meet you at the Inn."

"We'll be there long before you are," laughed Daddy, as he and Honey Bunch climbed aboard one of the toboggans.

It had taken them about half an hour to reach the hill. By going on the toboggan, he and Honey Bunch would get back to Snowtop Inn in less than ten minutes! The little girl sat down in front of her father. She held on very tightly to his legs which were stretched out on either side of her.

Mr. Morton, like the other riders, held onto a rope on either side of the toboggan so he could help to steer. Honey Bunch was wedged in so tightly between her father and a nice fat man in front of her that she couldn't possibly fall off the long sled.

"Everybody ready?" the man in charge called out. "All right, then, here we go!"

Down the hill raced the toboggan. Honey Bunch was sure she had never gone so fast in her life. At first she shut her eyes tightly. When she finally opened them, all she could see was the back of the man who was in front of her. Every time they went over a bump, Honey Bunch's face would be buried in his back.

"It's a good thing he's so nice and soft," she giggled to herself, "or my poor nose might get broken!"

The little girl peeked out once, but the wind stung her eyes so badly that she quickly pulled her head behind the man again.

Around the corners they flew! Whenever they turned left, the driver would yell "Left!" Everyone would lean to that side and pull on the right rope. Honey Bunch leaned over with everyone else.

"Oh, that was fun!" she cried, when they came to a stop at the foot of the hill.

"Did you know that you helped to steer the toboggan?" Daddy asked her. "When all of us put our weight on one side, we made it go in that direction."

Honey Bunch was thrilled to think she had helped to steer the big toboggan and could hardly wait to tell Stub.

"What would you like to do now?" Mr. Morton asked her. "I must go up to the Inn to make a telephone call. How about staying here and watching the skaters?"

The toboggan run had ended near a small pond on which only children were skating. Honey Bunch decided this must be the little lake reserved for boys and girls staying at Snowtop Inn. It was separated from the big lake by a high mound of snow.

"Yes, I'd like to watch them," Honey Bunch replied. "I'll stay right here, Daddy, until you come back."

After Mr. Morton had gone, the little girl ran up and down the shore of the pond, watching the children skate. There were a good many of them, but only a few could skate well.

"I wish Mitzi were here," Honey Bunch thought. "She could give me a lesson." But Mitzi was not around.

Honey Bunch walked up toward the narrow end of the pond where Billy Allen was doing a few fancy twists and turns on the ice. She could see he was a very good skater. Near him was Susan Jane Black, who could not skate very well. She was trying to make Billy show her how he skated backwards.

"Oh, you'd better stick to straight skating," Billy told her, as she tripped and fell on the ice.

Susan Jane did not like to be told this. As Billy skated off, she called out:

"I dare you to catch me!"

The wilful little girl started away to the roped off section of the pond. Honey Bunch knew no one was supposed to skate there. It was the very end of the pond where the fresh water flowed in and the ice was thin.

"Don't go there!" Billy called to Susan Jane, as she glided under the rope.

But Susan Jane paid no attention. She said something about him being a 'fraidy cat, and

84

went on. Billy skated under the rope and took her by the arm.

"You come back here!" he said. "You'll get into trouble!"

Susan Jane, instead of obeying him, took his hand and dragged him nearer the thin ice.

"Please, Susan Jane!" Billy cried out, trying to get the naughty girl back where it was safe.

Suddenly she pulled away from him, and laughing glided back toward the rope. Billy Allen started back too. At this moment there was a cracking sound. The ice on which he stood broke, and the little boy went down into the water!

"Oh!" screamed Susan Jane.

In a moment Billy stood up and tried to pull himself onto the ice. His fingers slipped and once more he disappeared beneath the water.

Honey Bunch knew she must do something to help him, and do it quickly!

Across the mound of snow was the big lake with the grownup skaters. She would try to get one of the men to help Billy!

CHAPTER VIII

THE MAGIC DINNER

"Rudy! Rudy!" Honey Bunch cried, as she reached the top of the mound of snow.

The skating instructor was just below her, giving a lesson. He looked up as Honey Bunch called out:

"Come quick! Billy's in the water and he can't get out!"

Rudy did not wait to hear any more. As if he had wings, he jumped up the mound of snow.

"Where?" he cried, pausing just a second.

"Over there!" Honey Bunch pointed. "Where the ice broke!"

Rudy made a flying leap from the top of the snow mound and landed on the firm ice. Then he skated beneath the rope onto the thin ice. It cracked under his weight and he landed in the water, but this did not matter for he was very tall.

In a few moments he had waded over to Billy. He lifted the boy in his arms and walked through the water to the bank of the pond, breaking the ice as he went.

Honey Bunch had run over to meet them. "Are you—are you all right, Billy?" she cried out.

"I'm c-cold," he said, his teeth chattering. He was not able to stand up.

By this time many children had gathered around and several grownups had come from the big lake. One of them took off Billy's skates. Another offered his coat, put it around the boy, and carried him to the hotel. Billy was made to get into a tub of hot water, and then go to bed for several hours.

Susan Jane stayed in her own room. It can be said to her credit that she was ashamed of what she had done.

Honey Bunch received a great deal of praise for her quick action. The boy might have been drowned if it had not been for her! But she did not think about this; she was so glad that Billy was all right.

During the rest of the day she and Stub played outdoors. Then late in the afternoon, Mother said it was time to get dressed for supper.

"May we eat in the children's dining room?" Honey Bunch asked her.

"Yes, indeed. And from what I heard this afternoon, you will enjoy it very much." Mrs. Morton smiled rather mysteriously, but she would tell no more.

The two little girls put on their next-to-the-prettiest dresses which they had brought with them. Stub's was a red and white flowered print, and Mrs. Morton tied a red ribbon on her hair. Honey Bunch put on a light blue dress trimmed with dark blue velvet.

"You both look very nice," said Mrs. Morton, as the children started for the hall.

Honey Bunch closed the door behind them. Stub, who had gone out first, did not walk toward the elevator. Instead, she turned the other way toward the end of the hall.

"That's the wrong way," Honey Bunch reminded her.

Stub said she wanted to go down the back stairway. That was the way Honey Bunch had gone to the laundry, and Stub thought it would be fun to see what it was like.

When the cousins reached the first floor, they heard voices on the other side of the door which

88

opened into the hall. Someone was crying.

"Bu-but I don't like Susan Jane and I don't want to be her friend," a little boy sobbed. Honey Bunch recognized Billy Allen's voice.

"That's not a nice thing to say, dear," a woman answered him. The little girls were sure she was Billy's aunt, Miss Allen. "You must be polite to all the little girls at Snowtop Inn."

Stub reached out to open the door, but Honey Bunch pulled her back.

"Don't!" she said. "It wouldn't be nice for them to know we heard them."

Honey Bunch and Stub stood still thinking Miss Allen and Billy would move away. Instead, they stayed right there. Suddenly Billy said:

"But Honey Bunch saved my life! I want her to be my partner the day of the big party."

Honey Bunch wondered what he meant, but she did not wait to find out. The Allens must not know she and Stub had heard what they had been saying. Quickly she took Stub by the hand and pulled her up the stairs.

"We'll go back and come down in the elevator," she said.

All the way to the dining room Honey Bunch

kept thinking about what Billy had said; that he wanted her for his partner the day of the big party. What could he have meant?

The little girl might have kept on thinking about it longer, but in a moment they reached the children's dining room, and she forgot it for the time being.

What an attractive place the children's dining room was! From the ceiling hung balloons of many colors. The walls were painted with pictures of familiar stories. Here was Humpty-Dumpty. Next to him was Simple Simon and the Pieman. Honey Bunch could pick out nearly all the nursery rhymes.

The head waitress smiled at Honey Bunch and Stub and took them to a table near the wall.

"This is the first time you have been here, so perhaps you would like to sit at this table to-night," she said. "When you have made some friends, you will probably want to sit with them."

The cousins sat down. They could not remember the names of the children at their table, though they had met them that morning at the dancing class. They were glad Susan Jane was not among them.

The waitress brought them some soup. A boy named Donny, who was directly across the table, asked Honey Bunch and Stub if they would like some salt. Before they could answer, he picked up the salt shaker, which was in the shape of a duck, then set it down again. At once the shaker began to waddle across the table. As it reached Honey Bunch's place, the duck stopped and said:

"Quack!"

The little girls laughed merrily. Donny explained that he had pressed a button on the duck's wing to make him perform. Then the child next to Honey Bunch, whose name was Betty, said:

"You won't need any sugar tonight, but at breakfast we use it and have lots of fun with the sugar bowl."

"Please show us what you mean," said Stub.

Betty picked up the bowl and set it down in front of Stub. "Take off the lid," she directed.

Stub did this, and at once music began to come from the bowl. It was a very pretty tune.

"Isn't this place fun?" said Honey Bunch. "Do they have any more tricks in the dining room?"

Instead of answering, Donny said "Look out!"

It was too late for Honey Bunch to look out. A shower of sugar fell on her, some of it going on her curls, some down her neck. Stub had wanted to find out what made the music play. She had held the bowl up high, and then let it turn upside down, so all the sugar spilled out on her cousin.

Betty giggled, but got up to help Honey Bunch shake the sugar from her hair. Stub, who was sorry about what had happened, helped too.

"We ought to call you Sugar Bunch instead of Honey Bunch," Betty said, and everyone laughed, including Honey Bunch.

The nice waitress cleaned up the sugar with a cloth and a brush.

"I'm glad you didn't break the bowl," she said to Stub. "It would be hard to get another like it."

Stub promised to be careful after this, and ate the rest of her supper without any more accidents.

While they were eating their main course, Donny told the cousins that each evening there was a surprise made by Wilbur, the chef.

"Everyone has to be ready for dessert before we can see it," he told Honey Bunch and Stub. "So you'd better hurry and finish."

A little later a great hush came over the dining room. The children seated near the pantry door had seen the chef coming, and instantly they had stopped talking. Then those at the next table became quiet, and so on until everyone in the dining room was still.

Wilbur was a very tall man, and he wore a very tall white chef's hat. The top of it almost touched the balloons. He was pushing a cart, and he stopped when he reached the center of the dining room.

"Good evening," he said, smiling. Then he looked around the room. Wilbur always did this to find out where any newcomers were seated. Now he saw Honey Bunch and Stub and bowed low to them. "I am glad to welcome you to the secrets of Snowtop," he told them.

The chef now opened the cart, took out a long cord, and asked Donny to attach one end of it to an electric outlet. Then he brought out the biggest mixing bowl Honey Bunch had ever seen. She wished Mrs. Miller, their laundress at home, might see it.

"She could make millions of cookies in it!" Honey Bunch thought.

Next the man removed a box of eggs from inside his cart and opened a whole dozen of them into the bowl. He asked the children to count the eggs as he cracked them. Next he put in sugar and vanilla, then poured in several quarts of cream and milk.

Back inside the cart went the big bowl. The chef clicked a little switch, and the children heard a whirring sound like bees on the wing.

A few minutes later a waitress came from the pantry with a tray full of sauce dishes and set them down on a table near Wilbur. She looked at the clock on the wall and whispered something to him. He nodded, and said aloud:

"Suppose you little ladies and gentlemen come up here one by one and see what I have. Each of you take one of these dishes, and I'll fill it for you. Since it is our custom to serve newcomers first, will the little Morton girls step to the front of the line?"

Honey Bunch and Stub slid from their chairs and walked across the room. Honey Bunch was eager to see what the chef had, but Stub was sure she did not want any of the soupy milk and egg

94

mixture to eat. The man lifted out the big bowl and set it on top of the cart.

"Ice cream!" cried Honey Bunch in delight, as she looked inside.

Sure enough! Wilbur's magic machine had beaten and frozen the eggs and milk in a few minutes. The chef heaped Honey Bunch's dish high and said:

"We call this frozen eggnog."

The little girl was sure she had never tasted better ice cream. She decided that whenever she ate in a restaurant, she would order frozen eggnog. Stub was very much surprised at what had happened to the milk and eggs, and ate every speck of her dessert.

After supper the cousins ran off to tell Mr. and Mrs. Morton about the wonderful dining room. Honey Bunch's parents said that nothing so exciting had happened at their dinner, and they wished they could be children again.

"But I have a surprise, too," announced Daddy Morton. "Tomorrow morning Santa Ross is going to drive us over to the Vasas' home."

Honey Bunch and Stub were very much pleased to hear this. They looked forward to seeing Christina and her brother Axel. Maybe Axel would dance for them!

The Mortons got up early the next day to be ready for the trip. As soon as breakfast was over and Mother had made sure the children had washed their hands and brushed their teeth, she helped them into their outdoor clothes.

Santa Ross was waiting at the front door of Snowtop Inn with the same sleigh and horses which had met them at the station. Before climbing in, Honey Bunch and Stub patted the animals. They giggled as they saw the steam coming from the horses' noses.

"It's like steam from a train," said Honey Bunch. "I guess the sleigh is our steam horse train."

"That's a good name for it," smiled Santa Ross as Honey Bunch climbed in beside him. "Only our steam horse train will make its own tracks in the snow."

Honey Bunch said this was a good thing. Then they could not get lost, because they could follow the tracks when they came back. Santa Ross said she was a very bright little girl to think of this. He told her if she ever should get lost, he knew she could find her way home.

As they drove along, the horses climbed up one long hill after another. Honey Bunch wondered how high up the Vasas' house was. She had been sure Snowtop Inn was on the very top of the world, but now she knew she had been wrong.

"Christina must live on the *tip* top of the world," she said.

"She certainly does," Santa Ross agreed. "You see that evergreen woods way up there? We have to drive through that. The Vasas' house is on the other side of it."

When the Mortons' steam horse train finally came out of the woods, they saw a large, attractive cabin ahead of them. It was one story high and built entirely of big logs.

"Oh, it's the nicest house I ever saw!" cried Honey Bunch.

As the sleigh stopped, they could hear sweet musical notes, which seemed to come from the other side of the cabin. Honey Bunch asked what they were.

"Axel must be practicing on his *luren*," said Santa Ross.

CHAPTER IX

FEEDING THE BIRDS

"WHAT is a *luren?*" Stub asked Santa Ross.
"A very long horn," said the driver. "It is played in northern Sweden where the Vasas come from."

As the Mortons got out of the sleigh, the door of the log cabin opened and Christina ran out.

"I'm so glad you're here," she cried, and gave Honey Bunch and Stub each a hug.

The cousins thought Christina looked prettier than ever. Her dress was different from any child's dress they had ever seen, and Honey Bunch supposed it was one of her costumes from Sweden.

At this moment a boy came around the side of the cabin. He was very handsome, and they all knew at once he must be Christina's brother Axel. In his hand he carried a horn. It was five feet long! As tall as he was!

After he had met the Mortons, Stub asked him to play the horn. Holding it to his mouth, he blew on it for several minutes. Then Stub said she would like to play the *luren*. Axel handed it over, and the little girl tried very hard to make sweet musical notes come from it, but she could not get a sound.

Honey Bunch took a turn, but she could not do any better than her cousin. The little girl thought it was too bad that Norman Clark couldn't be there to try blowing it. He surely could make some noise come from the *luren!* Mrs. Miller always said that Norman could make more noise than any boy she had ever known.

Christina asked the little girls into the house to meet her mother. Mrs. Vasa was a plump, pretty woman. She wore a large white apron with beautiful lace around the edge of it. She greeted Honey Bunch and Stub with a smile and drew them to her.

"I am glad to meet you, my dears," she said. "Christina has told me so much about you."

Christina showed the visitors her home. The fine hand-carved furniture had been brought from Sweden, she said, and her mother had made the rugs on a hand loom. Honey Bunch and Stub thought they were very beautiful, although they were quite different from those at their homes. Christina told them Mrs. Vasa also had embroidered the blue and red designs on the curtains at the windows, and had crocheted all the bedspreads. The one in Christina's room had a lovely pattern showing Swedish children at play.

"I like everything," said Stub. "I'm going to tell my mother all about your house."

Mr. Vasa came in from his workshop. Honey Bunch thought his blue eyes sparkled more than ever. She wondered if living high up near the blue sky had anything to do with it, and asked him this.

"Perhaps it does," he laughed. "My hair is beginning to turn silver. Do you suppose that comes from making silver jewelry?"

He and Honey Bunch laughed together at this. Then the man led her to his workshop. Stub and Mr. and Mrs. Morton followed. It was a large room with long tables and benches and many pieces of machinery. On one wall hung several photographs. Honey Bunch asked if they were pictures of the jewelry Mr. Vasa had made.

"No," he said. "They are photographs of

100

something you'd never think of. Snowflakes."

"Snowflakes!" Honey Bunch and Stub cried out together.

Mr. Vasa explained it was fun to take pictures of snowflakes. He invited all the Mortons to come over sometime when it was snowing and watch how he did it.

"You see, no two snowflakes are alike in design. But you will notice," he added, pointing to the photographs on the wall, "that every snowflake is made up of six parts. Each part is exactly like the others."

"Why do we have to wait until it is snowing to see some flakes?" Stub asked.

Mr. Vasa explained that the snowflakes stuck together when they fell on the ground. To get a picture of a snowflake, he had to catch a single falling flake on a piece of iced glass. Then he looked at it at once under a microscope before the snowflake could melt.

"When I see a design I like, I photograph it immediately," the jeweler said. "Perhaps when you girls look at some you'll find designs you like. If you do, I'll make silver pins for you just like the snowflakes."

Honey Bunch and Stub thought the man was

101

very kind. They wished it would start snowing right away! But the sun was shining brightly, and there was not a snow cloud in the sky.

"Let's go outdoors," said Christina.

Her father wanted to talk business with Mr. Morton, and Mrs. Vasa and Mrs. Morton were busy looking at some handmade handkerchiefs. Axel went outside with the girls and led the way to a large barn. In it were horses, wagons, sleighs, and a long narrow wooden sled which Axel said was a log sled.

"When we need firewood we just go out in the woods for our logs, and cart them back on this sled," he said.

"Would you like to play some games?" Christina asked. "Or maybe you'd like to see Axel dance."

"Oh, I'd love to see you dance, Axel," said Honey Bunch. "Please do some of the steps you learned in Sweden."

Axel blushed. Though he loved to dance, he did not like to show off. But Honey Bunch coaxed him so long, he finally gave in. The three little girls sat down on some hay, and Axel did several folk dance steps. Suddenly he stopped.

"Oh, it's no good without music," he said.

Stub giggled. "I couldn't do that dance even with music," she stated. Then she added, "Honey Bunch is a wonderful dancer, too. I bet she could do the steps."

Christina insisted Honey Bunch get up and try them. Axel was very willing to show her, and he was amazed how fast she learned the steps. Honey Bunch was pleased herself that she had not made many mistakes.

"I just love this dance," she told Axel. "When I get home I'm going to ask my dancing teacher to show it to all the boys and girls."

Stub wanted to see the other buildings, so the four children walked outside once more. Stub spied a little square house built on stilts high above the ground.

"What is that for?" she asked.

"That's our storehouse," Axel explained. "We built it high so it won't get buried in the snow. We keep lots of food in it."

Stub had noticed a ladder leading to the door of the storehouse. At once she wanted to climb up and look inside. Without waiting for the others, she started up the rungs of the ladder. Now Stub lived on a farm and was used to going

103

up and down a ladder to the haymow. But haymow ladders are kept indoors and never get icy. The ladder Stub was on at this moment was very different. Snow had fallen on the rungs and then frozen. Now they were very, very slippery.

Before the little girl knew what was happening, her feet slipped from under her. She lost her balance and slid between two of the rungs. Plop! she landed in a heap in the deep snow.

The other children ran to her side, but Stub was not hurt. Her snowsuit was heavy and she was well padded, and the deep snow was soft.

"We always put on special shoes when we climb to the storehouse," said Christina. "They have spikes on them and our feet don't slip. I'll get you some if you like, Stub."

But Stub had lost her curiosity about what was inside the building. At this moment she and the others became interested in a flock of birds which had flown over from the woods near by.

"They're coming here for food," said Axel. "Would you like to help feed them?"

Honey Bunch and Stub liked this idea. As they went toward the house to get the food, Mr. Vasa came out with a pan of seed. Honey Bunch noticed that more and more birds were appearing. Some hopped along the ground, while others sat on the branches of trees near the house.

"I guess these birds forgot to go South," said Honey Bunch to Mr. Vasa. She remembered that Mrs. Miller, the laundress at home, had said she would like to go South in the winter as birds do.

Christina's father explained that there are many birds which do not go South in the wintertime. "In fact," he said, "some birds prefer living where it is cold all ʏ ʏr round. When it gets warm here in the summer, they fly even farther North where it never gets warm."

Honey Bunch was surprised to hear this. To be sure, she had seen a few birds in Barham in the wintertime, but she had no idea so many different birds liked the snow.

"You see that tiny little one over there?" Mr. Vasa asked her. "That's a snow bunting. When he sings, some people in Canada think he says 'Swe-e-et Can-a-da, Can-a-da, Can-a-da,' so *they* call him the Canada bird."

Mr. Vasa also pointed out a nuthatch and a brown creeper. He said he sometimes saw owls in the winter. They were called snowy owls.

105

One little gray bird with long white feathers on each side of his tail hopped right up to the group. Mr. Vasa said this was a junco, the most friendly of all the winter birds.

"When juncos are hungry, they'll eat bread crumbs or most anything we give them. But they like seeds best of all," he told the little girls.

"Oh, look!" cried Christina, pointing upward. "Here come the snowflakes!"

"But they're not snow. They're birds," said Stub.

"That's right," agreed Mr. Vasa, "but just watch them. They look like falling snow."

A flock of the birds started to come down. They were pure white underneath, and as they floated to the earth fluttering their wings nervously, they looked just like falling snow.

"Yes, they do look like snowflakes," Honey Bunch said. "And aren't they darling!"

Several of the birds came near the cabin to eat the seeds, but many of them were too shy and remained in the trees. Christina said they would come down after everyone had gone into the house.

Suddenly there was a great commotion among the birds on the other side of the cabin. Those in the trees began to scream and chatter. The ones on the ground near Honey Bunch instantly flew away.

"What happened?" she asked excitedly.

Mr. Vasa did not answer. Instead, he called out:

"Axel! Axel! Blow them out!"

CHAPTER X

THE SNOWMAN CONTEST

WHEN Axel's father cried "Blow them out!" the boy ran to get his *luren*. Holding the horn to his mouth, he blew on it strongly, filling the air with sweet sounds. The birds stopped their noise and flew away.

In the meantime, Mr. Vasa had run to the front of the cabin. Honey Bunch went after him, and was just in time to see the end of a sad bird fight. Two birds with long, sharp bills had been pecking madly at two smaller birds, but now the big ones flew away.

"Those bigger ones are shrikes," said Mr. Vasa. "They are very mean birds and sometimes they bite off the heads of the smaller birds."

"How dreadful!" Honey Bunch cried.

"That's why I told Axel to blow his *luren*," the man explained. "The shrikes are afraid of the noise. Whenever I hear a commotion, I'm pretty sure those bad birds are around."

Honey Bunch asked why the other birds did not fly away before the shrikes could start a fight. She was told that the shrikes are very clever and can imitate other birds. They pretend to be the kind of bird which they want to attack. Often they imitate snowflakes. Then, when it is too late, the poor snowflakes find a stranger in their midst trying to bite their heads off!

"Birds have their troubles just like people, don't they?" sighed Honey Bunch. "Sometimes people get their heads bitten off by other people."

Mr. Vasa looked surprised. "What do you mean by that?" he asked, puzzled. "I never heard of such a thing."

"I'm sure they do," said Honey Bunch, "'cause one time our milkman was afraid Mrs. Miller was going to bite his head off. She's our laundress. He left our milk in the sun and it got sour. She scolded him and he said, 'Well, you don't have to bite my head off!'"

Mr. Vasa laughed until he shook all over. Then he patted Honey Bunch and explained this was only a way of saying you thought somebody was scolding you too hard.

Mr. and Mrs. Morton came from the cabin just then and told Honey Bunch it was time to start back to Snowtop Inn. Santa Ross, who had gone off to get some evergreen boughs to put in the hotel lobby, returned with the sleigh.

"Come again soon," Mrs. Vasa invited them all. "Sometime when you come we shall have a Swedish dinner."

Christina and Axel waved to Honey Bunch and Stub until they were out of sight. On the drive to the hotel, Santa Ross let both little girls hold the reins. Stub was better at this than Honey Bunch because she lived on a farm and often helped her daddy drive. But Honey Bunch tried hard to keep the animals in the roadway.

."Am I keeping our steam horse train on the track all right?" she asked Santa Ross.

The man assured her she was, but he took the reins as they neared Snowtop Inn. He let them out at the front door. The children ran ahead into the lobby. Many of the guests were crossing it on their way to luncheon. Betty, the little girl who had sat next to Honey Bunch in the children's dining room the night before, came up to them.

110

"Oh, you missed the announcement this morning," she said. "Where did you go?"

Honey Bunch explained where they had been. Then she asked what the announcement was.

"Every family has to make a snowman this afternoon," Betty told her. "I mean, every family that wants to. You want to, don't you?"

"Oh, yes," said Honey Bunch. "I'm sure Daddy and Mother will, too. I'll tell them about it."

Mr. and Mrs. Morton thought the snowman was a fine idea, but Mother said she guessed she would let Daddy and the girls make him. Mr. Morton went to the hotel desk and asked what the rules were for the contest, because he knew it must be a contest.

"Yes, there are some rules," the clerk told him. "You are supposed to make your snowman look as much like someone connected with the hotel as you possibly can. You are not to tell anyone who it is. The judges will announce the winners at eight-thirty tonight."

By three o'clock that afternoon, about fifteen families were lined up along the lake ready for their work. The fathers were joking among themselves, and many of the children already were rolling up snow into big balls to start making their snowmen.

"Well, Honey Bunch and Stub," said Daddy Morton, "who is *our* snowman going to look like?"

At first neither of them could think of a person. Then suddenly Honey Bunch danced around and clapped her hands. She was sure she knew just the right one.

"We'll make our snowman look like Santa Ross!" she cried out.

Now Honey Bunch did not notice that Susan Jane Black was going by at the moment, or she would not have spoken so loudly. The unpleasant little girl smiled to herself. She knew who the Mortons' snow statue would be!

"They'll never win a prize, 'cause they're not following the rules," she thought.

The girl hurried on to where Mr. Black was ready to start work. He asked her who their snowman was going to be.

"I think we ought to make a statue of the clerk at the desk," Susan Jane said to her father. "Everybody likes him, so we ought to get first prize."

"If I can make a chunk of snow look like the

112

desk clerk, it'll be more than I expect, Sue. I'm no artist," Mr. Black laughed. He was not unpleasant like his daughter.

"You just have to, Father. I want the first prize," Susan Jane said peevishly.

Some distance away the Mortons were not thinking about the prize. They were having a very good time making their snowman, but it was hard work. It took nearly an hour to pile up the snow for the body and shape out arms and a head.

Daddy Morton was just about to start carving out the face, when Honey Bunch called his attention to a man skating toward them on the ice. He was pushing a big sled with a huge metal box on it.

"It's Wilbur!" cried the little girl. "I know, 'cause he has on his high white hat."

"But not his white suit," said Stub, as she too recognized the chef from the children's dining room. The man had on a black skisuit and skates!

When Wilbur reached the Mortons, he stopped and smiled. The children could see steam coming from the metal box. The chef opened it and a delicious aroma came out!

113

"Would you like some tomato soup and steak sandwiches?" he asked.

The children and Mr. Morton said they certainly would. Honey Bunch remarked she had never eaten out-of-doors on top of the world and it would be fun. Wilbur handed them cups of soup and hot buns with slices of broiled steak inside.

"I'll pick up the cups on my way back," he said. "Hm," the chef remarked as he started off, "that's a nice snowman."

Honey Bunch and Stub thought so too. As soon as they finished the delicious food, they began smoothing out the snowman's arms as Daddy Morton had told them to do. Pretty soon he finished the face.

"Well, does that look like Santa Ross?"

"Ye-yes," said Honey Bunch slowly. To be truthful, she was just a little disappointed. "But, Daddy," she went on, "isn't his nose too big? Santa Ross's is littler and rounder like Santa Claus's."

"I believe you're right," Mr. Morton agreed. "But I don't know what size to make it."

"I'll find out," offered Honey Bunch.

Before Daddy could say anything, she ran off.

Stub went after her, but had a hard time catching her cousin.

"Where are you going?" she asked, panting.

"To the stables. I'm sure Santa Ross is there and I want to see how big his nose is," Honey Bunch replied.

As they rushed into the building, they almost ran into Santa Ross. He was just starting to feed the horses.

"May I please measure your nose?" Honey Bunch asked him excitedly.

Santa Ross stood still and stared at the little girl. "What did you say?" he asked.

Stub tried to explain. "We're making you in snow and my uncle has to know how big your nose is," she said.

Now Santa Ross had not heard of the snowman contest, so he could not figure out what the children meant. But after a few minutes' talk with them, he said:

"Oh, now I see what you're driving at. Well, that's very nice to make a snow statue of me. Let's see. How can we measure my nose?"

"I know," said Honey Bunch. "Please stand here by this stool."

She climbed onto it and stood up. This way

115

the little girl could reach the man's head. She laid her fingers one after the other along his nose from his forehead to the end of it. It was just the length of her middle finger. And across the base of it, Santa Ross's nose was just the length of Honey Bunch's little finger.

"Thank you very much," she said, jumping down from the stool.

"I want to measure your mouth," said Stub. "We ought to know about your mouth."

But it was impossible to do this. Though Stub tried over and over again, Santa Ross could not keep from laughing and this made his mouth several different sizes.

"I guess we'll just have to get along without your mouth," sighed Stub, and got down.

The cousins ran back to Mr. Morton and told him they knew the exact size of the sleigh driver's nose. He grinned when he heard how they had found out. Daddy held his small daughter in his arms, so she could lay her fingers on top of the snowman's nose.

"You were right," Daddy Morton told her when she was through measuring. "I'll make Santa Ross's nose smaller right away."

After he finished, Honey Bunch was sure the

snowman looked just like the person he was
supposed to be. She did hope the judges would
know he was nice Santa Ross!

As it had begun to grow dark, floodlights were
turned on the scene. The Mortons could see the
long line of snowmen clearly now. Some of
them were very fine looking indeed, but the
Mortons did not recognize any of the figures.

"I guess that's 'cause we haven't been here
long enough to know everybody," Honey Bunch
told her Daddy.

They started back to the hotel, and met
Mother, who was just coming to get them. She
thought the girls should eat in the children's
dining room where supper would be served
early this evening.

"Then you can take naps afterwards and be
ready to go outside at eight-thirty," she said.

The cousins quickly changed their clothes
and went to the dining room. The only two
vacant places were directly across from where
Susan Jane Black and Billy Allen were sitting
side by side. During the meal Billy leaned
across and said:

"I hope you win one of the prizes, Honey
Bunch. I saw your snowman. It's good!"

Honey Bunch smiled and started to thank the boy, when Susan Jane spoke up. Her voice was so loud every child in the dining room could hear her.

"The Mortons can't win a prize!" she said.

"Why not?" asked Billy.

"'Cause they didn't follow the rules!"

"We did too!" exclaimed Stub.

Susan Jane insisted they had not, but she would not tell why. During the rest of the meal she kept giggling and whispering first to Betty, who sat on one side of her, and then to Billy on the other.

Honey Bunch was very uncomfortable and she was worried, too. She did not mind if they did not win a prize, but she was sorry that her father had put so much work on a snowman that could not be in the contest. She did not want all the people at Snowtop to think they had not followed the rules.

When the cousins went upstairs for their naps, Stub lay down at once and fell sound asleep. But Honey Bunch lay wide-awake thinking about what Susan Jane had said. What had she meant?

An hour later Mrs. Morton came to awaken

118

the children. To her surprise Honey Bunch was not there. Stub, rubbing her eyes sleepily, said she did not know where her cousin was.

"She was right on that bed last time I saw her," Stub told her aunt.

Mrs. Morton thought Honey Bunch would show up any minute, but she did not come. It was not like her little daughter to go off without telling anyone. Something must have happened to her!

CHAPTER XI

FANCY SKATERS

WHEN Daddy Morton heard that Honey Bunch was missing, he looked all over the hotel for her, but he could not find her. He came back to the room to tell Mother and Stub. Just then, a band began to play outside.

"Oh, please, may I go out and see the band?" asked Stub. She was worried about her cousin, but she knew Honey Bunch usually took care of herself well, and probably was not in trouble.

"All right, dear, you may go out," said her Aunt Edith.

She helped the little girl into her warm clothes, and told her not to go far away.

Stub ran to the elevator, and of course stubbed her toe just as she got into it, and fell flat on the floor. A friendly man helped her up and laughingly said he did not blame her for being in a hurry.

"I suppose you heard the music, too," he said. "It's going to be a lot of fun out there."

120

Stub thought so too, but said it would be more fun if her cousin were not lost. Everyone in the elevator wanted to know all about it. When they heard about Honey Bunch, they all looked concerned.

"I hope she didn't go outside," said one of the women. "There are so many places where a child could get lost in the snow."

Stub wished the lady had not said this. It was bad enough having Honey Bunch gone. Stub had felt sure she would turn up soon, but now maybe Honey Bunch really was in danger!

Not knowing what else to do, Stub followed the other people outside. The band which had been playing near the front door had started to march toward the lake. Stub hurried and caught up to the man who was leading the band. Suddenly a little distance in front of her, she saw another child.

"Why, it's Honey Bunch!" she cried aloud.

Stub was so excited she ran ahead of the band. She went so fast she fell down two different times, but Stub did not mind this. She had found her cousin!

"Honey Bunch! Honey Bunch!" she cried. "Your daddy and mother are dreadfully worried about you. Why did you come out here?"

Honey Bunch did not seem to hear her cousin. She looked very sad standing beside the Santa Ross snowman.

"What's the matter with you?" Stub asked her abruptly.

Honey Bunch quickly explained she was worried about what Susan Jane had said. Stub was surprised to hear this, for she knew Susan Jane was not a nice little girl and she could not understand why Honey Bunch paid attention to her.

"Well, you'd better go back and tell your mother and daddy where you've been," Stub advised. "They're worried about you. I bet they think you froze to death."

When Honey Bunch heard this, she ran off as fast as her legs could take her. She met her parents near the front door of the Inn. They were just starting to search for her outside.

"Oh, I'm awfully, awfully sorry I went away," Honey Bunch cried, hugging them both. "I wanted to see our snowman all alone, before he was put out of the contest."

She explained what Susan Jane had said. Daddy Morton stated that Susan Jane was a troublesome child, and he would put no stock in her words. Honey Bunch felt better when she heard this. She held her daddy's hand very tightly.

"Mrs. Miller always says that," she told him.

"Says what?" Mr. Morton asked.

"That she puts no stock in things," Honey Bunch replied. "I never knew what she meant. You mean Susan Jane doesn't know what she's talking about?"

"I'm sure she doesn't," Mrs. Morton spoke up firmly.

Upon reaching the place where the snowmen were lined up, the Mortons stood still to listen to the music. The band had stopped marching, but the men went right on playing. Honey Bunch and Stub liked the lively tune and could not keep their feet still. Presently someone called out:

"Here come the judges!"

Everyone became quiet. There were three judges—two men and a woman. They had little notebooks in their hands. After they had looked over each snowman carefully, they wrote something down in them.

When they came to the Santa Ross statue, the three laughed heartily. Honey Bunch felt very funny inside. She was sure the snowman was very good. She wondered why the judges laughed at it.

They passed on to the last group, and made notes. Then they closed their little books, and handed them over to a man who was in charge of the contest. Honey Bunch was very much excited.

Presently the man walked over to the band leader. All the musicians stopped playing except the drummer. This man beat very hard and loud on his instrument.

"It sounds like thunder," Honey Bunch remarked. "It's the only kind of thunder we have in the wintertime, isn't it, Daddy?"

When the drum stopped rolling, the man who held the judges' notebooks began speaking.

"Ladies and Gentlemen," he said, "and Boys and Girls! Snowtop Inn wishes to thank you all for taking part in the Snowman Contest. Evidently there is a great deal of hidden talent among our guests." He paused a moment.

The grownups laughed, but Honey Bunch and Stub wished he would hurry up and tell them who had won the prizes. Finally he pulled a paper from his pocket and said:

"There are fifteen snowmen in the contest. The judges think one of them is a very good likeness of someone at the hotel." Then he laughed. "But even they might have guessed wrong. In order to be perfectly fair, I shall ask that someone from the family which made that particular snow statue come forward and tell us who it is."

He looked up and down the long line of snow-men and at the people who were standing beside them. Then, clearing his throat, he said loudly:

"Will Honey Bunch Morton please come this way?"

The little girl was so surprised she could hardly move. Stub gave her a little shove.

"Go on," her cousin urged. "Maybe you'll win a prize."

As Honey Bunch walked toward the man, she kept thinking about what Susan Jane had said; that they had not followed the rules. Maybe the judges had guessed the Mortons' statue looked like somebody totally different from the one he was supposed to be!

Suddenly the little girl spied Santa Ross standing off at a little distance. Quickly she dashed over to the sleigh driver and pulled him forward. He had heard the announcement. Now he blushed very red, as she called out:

"This is the one! Santa Ross is our snowman!"

The crowd burst into laughter at the little girl's words. Everyone knew the jolly sleigh driver, and some of them even thought he looked like Santa Claus, but no one had ever thought of calling him Santa Ross before.

"Then our judges guessed right," the man in charge announced, "and I award first prize to the Morton family!"

He handed Honey Bunch a ball-shaped glass paper weight. As she looked inside it, she could see a small hotel. The man shook the glass for her and to Honey Bunch's amazement, tiny snowflakes whirled around the miniature building.

"Why, it's just like Snowtop Inn!" cried Honey Bunch, as she danced up and down with her prize.

All the people clapped with the exception of one little girl. This was Susan Jane, who had thought all the time the Mortons were making a statue of Santa Claus instead of Santa Ross. She was even more disappointed when the other prizes were awarded and her family did not receive one of them.

"Our evening's entertainment will end with a skating exhibition," said the announcer. "A brother and sister who live near here will show us how boys and girls in Sweden skate. I take great pleasure in introducing Christina and Axel Vasa."

"Oh, isn't that wonderful!" cried Honey Bunch. "Let's hurry so we can get in the front row and see them."

She and Stub were the first ones to reach the spot, and had a good view of the children skating. How graceful they were on the ice! First they skated together, then each one skated alone.

"Aren't they marvelous!" Honey Bunch heard one woman say.

"Very fine," agreed a man next to her.

Honey Bunch was proud to know these children. She told Stub they must go over and speak to them as soon as the performance was finished. Susan Jane Black, who always wanted to show off in front of people, also ran to make their acquaintance. But Axel and Christina merely thanked her when she praised their skating, and turned at once to their friends.

"Hello, Honey Bunch! Hello, Stub!" they both cried out.

At this Susan Jane made a face. She did not like it because the Vasa children paid no attention to her. She pushed Honey Bunch aside and started to talk to Axel and Christina.

"Oh, I think you are simply wonderful," she said. "I'd love to come to your home sometime. Won't you teach me how to skate?"

"Rudy is a very good teacher," Axel told her. He thought Susan Jane was very rude to interrupt them.

"Oh, I know you could teach me much better," Susan Jane insisted.

Christina thought the girl was rude too. "We always ask our parents' permission before we invite anybody to our house," she told Susan Jane.

Susan Jane became very angry. "I think you're horrid," she cried, and walked off.

Honey Bunch and Stub would have liked to stay with Axel and Christina longer, but Mrs. Morton came to remind them that it was past their bedtime. She congratulated the Vasa children on their fine performance, saying she had never seen young folks skate better.

128

"Mother always says all children could skate well if they would only practice," Axel said. "Oh, Mrs. Morton, I almost forgot to tell you. Father wants you all to come over to our house tomorrow."

"Tomorrow?"

"Yes, he thinks it will snow and he wants you to see the snowflakes under the microscope."

Honey Bunch thought this was very exciting and said, "Oh, please let's go."

Daddy Morton came up at this moment and the invitation was repeated. He too thought it would snow and said:

"Yes, we'll come. Thank your father very much, Axel."

The Mortons said good night to the Vasa children and went back to the Inn. As the little cousins were getting ready for bed, Honey Bunch tried to remember everything she had learned about snowflakes.

"They have six parts, but each part's just like every other part," she said aloud.

"And every snowflake is different from every other snowflake," said Stub. "That's how Mr. Vasa gets so many designs for his jewelry."

So many exciting things had been going on

129

lately that Honey Bunch had almost forgotten why the Mortons had come to Snowtop. She wondered how her daddy was getting along trying to find the men who were copying Mr. Vasa's jewelry. As she dropped off to sleep she also thought about the boxes of jewelry which had been lost. Had the messenger stolen them, or had he lost the boxes?

The little girls slept later than usual the next morning. When they came downstairs, the children's dining room was closed, so they ate with Mr. and Mrs. Morton. Jenny, the waitress, was glad to see them.

"I've missed you," she said, smiling. "You haven't been in here since the first morning you came to Snowtop. Do they serve better food in the other dining room?" she teased them.

Stub did not know she was teasing, and said seriously, "You don't have balloons in here, or walking salt shakers, or sugar bowls that play music."

"But we do have a nice black pussy cat," Jenny said.

The waitress had just noticed a big black cat which had walked into the room and was coming along the wall toward the Mortons' table.

130

The cat was not supposed to come into the dining room, and ordinarily Jenny would have shooed him out, but she decided to have some fun with the little girls. Honey Bunch's eyes opened wide when she saw the cat.

"She's just like my Lady Clare at home!" she exclaimed.

"Maybe she *is* Lady Clare," Jenny said, trying not to laugh.

"Oh, no!" said Honey Bunch quickly. "Lady Clare is all black. She doesn't have a white spot on the end of her tail like this pussy."

The cat brushed against Honey Bunch's legs and purred in a friendly way. The little girl bent down to talk to her. She knew just how to talk to cats. This one, whose name was Mouser, must have liked Honey Bunch very much for he sat beside her while she ate.

When she finished her breakfast, Honey Bunch picked the cat up in her arms and carried him to the lobby. Daddy asked her if she would like to take the cat to the stables.

"Is that where she belongs?" Honey Bunch asked.

"I don't know," Daddy replied, "but since her name is Mouser, I suppose she likes to catch mice. I'm sure there must be a lot of mice around the stables. I'm going down there anyway, and I thought you would like to go along."

Honey Bunch thought she might see Santa Ross there. When she told this to her daddy he said Santa Ross was the very person he was going to find.

"I want to see if he will drive us over to the Vasas' cabin," Mr. Morton said. "If you want to go to the stables, put on your warm clothes."

Honey Bunch carried Mouser to her room. While she and Stub were putting on their snow-suits, he jumped to the window sill and looked out.

"I guess there aren't any mice around here," said Stub, "so Mouser has nothing to do but look at the scenery."

"He can work down at the barn," Honey Bunch replied.

She picked up the cat and went into her daddy's bedroom. As soon as he was ready, she and Stub skipped along with him to the stables. Santa Ross was getting ready to drive to the station. The big sleigh with its team of horses was waiting for him. Mr. Morton explained why he had come.

"I'm very sorry I can't take you myself this morning," Santa Ross said, shaking his head, "but I can lend you a horse. You know how to drive, don't you, Mr. Morton?"

"Why, yes," Honey Bunch's daddy replied.

"Then I'll give you a cutter," Santa Ross told him.

Honey Bunch wondered what in the world the man meant. Was a cutter a horse that was a cut-up? She had once heard Mrs. Miller say that at times Norman was a great cut-up, and the little girl knew Mrs. Miller meant he played jokes on other people. But she could not imagine how a horse could play a joke.

"Maybe two horses are a cutter," she thought.

Finally she decided to find out, because her daddy and Santa Ross did not seem to be doing anything about getting the cutter. As she asked the question they laughed. The good-natured driver led her into the barn and pointed out a one-seated sleigh. The little girl was puzzled.

"But what does it cut?" she asked.

Santa Ross said he had never figured this out, but he supposed it cut through the snow. Anyway, just one horse pulled it, he told her, and a person could go very fast.

133

Mr. Morton asked whether it would not be too hard for one horse to pull the whole Morton family up the hill to the Vasas' cabin.

"I'll give you Mountain King," Santa Ross said. "He's good and strong, and can pull all of you."

Honey Bunch and Stub liked this name for a horse. They wanted to see him at once, so Joe, the stable boy, showed them where he was. The horse was all black and had a beautiful long mane.

"He's very gentle and never runs away," Joe told them.

Santa Ross said that when the Mortons were ready to leave, Joe would hook up Mountain King for them. About an hour later they started off in the cutter. Stub sat between her aunt and uncle. Honey Bunch climbed onto her mother's lap.

"Giddap!" cried Daddy, and they were off.

CHAPTER XII

SNOWFLAKE PICTURES

"IT'S starting to snow!" cried Honey Bunch half an hour later, clapping her hands.

A few flakes had begun to fall, and within a few minutes they were coming down thickly. The Mortons were about halfway to the Vasas' cabin. Daddy urged Mountain King to go a little faster, but of course he could not make him run uphill.

Once Honey Bunch stood up and looked back. The snow was coming down so heavily the sleigh's tracks were covered very quickly.

"If we should get lost," said the little girl, "we couldn't use our tracks to find the way back."

"That's right, so we'll have to watch carefully where we're going," Daddy replied.

In a little while the snow was so thick that the Mortons could hardly see where they were going. Daddy headed for the evergreen forest, which was near Axel and Christina's home. In the woods the trees grew close together, and not so much snow fell on the road. As soon as the Mortons came out on the other side, though, there were so many snowflakes in the air Honey Bunch and Stub could hardly see the house.

Christina heard the bells on the cutter and opened the door of the cabin. Her friends shook the snow from their clothes and went inside. Axel hurried out and drove the horse into the barn. There he wiped off Mountain King thoroughly and put a blanket over him so he would not catch cold.

Inside the house the Mortons had removed their wraps and gone to Mr. Vasa's workshop. One of the windows there was open several inches. Every few seconds some snowflakes would blow inside, and the jeweler would catch a single flake on a small piece of ice-cold glass. Instantly he would put it under his microscope and look at it.

A special kind of camera stood near by. If Mr. Vasa liked the design of the snowflake, he would photograph it at once.

"Good morning," he said, without interrupting his work. "The snowflakes seem particularly beautiful this morning. Come, I will

136

show you some of nature's loveliest work."

One by one the Mortons gazed into the microscope. When it was Honey Bunch's turn, she was amazed to see how large a snowflake looked. On the little piece of glass it measured hardly a quarter of an inch across, but under the microscope it seemed over an inch wide.

"Isn't it be-au—" Honey Bunch started to say. But before she could finish the snowflake was nothing but a tiny puddle of water.

"Here's another one," said Mr. Vasa, sliding a new snowflake under the microscope.

"Oh, that's pretty!" cried Honey Bunch. "It looks like six fairies!"

"What are they doing?" Stub asked.

Honey Bunch explained they were playing Ring-around-a-rosy. When Mr. Vasa heard this, he quickly set the camera in place and snapped a picture of the snowflake.

"This is the most unusual design I've seen in a long time!" he said, his eyes sparkling.

Later, when he developed the film and printed the picture of the snowflake, everyone declared Honey Bunch had been right. The design surely did look like six little fairies in a circle.

"I shall make you a pin to look like that

snowflake," the jeweler promised the little girl.
"And nobody else in the whole wide world will
have one like it."

Honey Bunch thanked the man. She was just
about to ask if he would make a pin for Stub
also, when he said to her little cousin:

"I shall make you a pretty pin too. And now
how would you children like to go with Axel
and bring in some firewood?"

The children were surprised to find that it
had stopped snowing, and that the sun was out.
The three little girls put on their snowsuits and
ran toward the barn. Axel was bringing out
the log sled. A large pony was pulling it, and
on the animal's feet were strange-looking ob-
jects.

"They look like snowshoes but they're funny,"
said Honey Bunch.

"They are snowshoes," Christina told her.
"Our pony would sink down deep in the snow
if he didn't wear them. We don't stay on the
road in the woods, and there are lots of holes
in the snow. He might step into one and break
a leg."

Axel said he thought the girls should put on
snowshoes too. Christina went back into the

house and took three pair from a closet. She also got some heavy moccasins and told her friends to take off their boots and put on the moccasins.

Honey Bunch thought of the pretty little moccasins which her friend Ida had given her as a going-away gift. They were quite different from these outdoor moccasins. These were not white and shiny like hers. They were tan and the leather was rough. But they were lined with lovely soft gray fur.

"How do we put on the snowshoes?" Stub asked. She thought they looked like great big tennis rackets, and wondered how she could ever keep them on her feet.

"I'll show you how," Christina offered.

Axel jumped from the log sled to help Honey Bunch with hers. He and Christina pulled the straps across the children's feet and buckled them tight.

"Now, when you walk, raise your feet very high," Axel told them. "And don't let the snowshoes get close together or you'll trip and fall."

As Honey Bunch started to move, she found it very hard to keep her feet far apart. It was not difficult to step up high, but she could not

seem to remember how to put her feet down
again. The snowshoes always came down on
top of each other. After she had fallen several
times and been helped up, she sighed and said:

"Oh, dear, I wish my legs grew far apart like
the pony's."

"You'd be a funny-looking girl if they did,"
giggled Stub, who was having troubles of her
own.

But after a little practice around the yard, the
cousins found that they could walk quite well on
the snowshoes. Axel asked them if they thought
they could go all the way to the woods and back
on them.

"We'll try," said Honey Bunch and Stub.

They started off, hoping to keep up with the
pony, but they soon found this was not possible.
He was not even three years old, but he could
walk on snowshoes much better than they could!

"Maybe he gets along better because he has
four feet," suggested Honey Bunch.

"You're not going to wish you had four feet!"
Stub teased her.

The little party was very gay as they went
down the hill to the evergreen forest. Honey
Bunch loved it inside the big woods. The snow-

birds twittered overhead, and twice she saw rabbits scurrying among the trees.

Presently Axel turned the pony off the main road and waited for the girls. He warned them to be careful of holes. Honey Bunch paid strict attention and did not get into any trouble. But Stub did not have such good luck. A hunter had set a small trap and Stub stepped squarely on top of it with one of her snowshoes.

Snap! went the trap. It knocked Stub completely off balance and she fell down. Honey Bunch tried to help her up, but when she leaned over she too lost her balance and went down.

Stub had not hurt herself, but the cousins found it impossible to stand up again with their snowshoes on. Christina and Axel helped them up, and the boy said the girls might as well rest for a while as he was not driving any farther.

"Are you going to get the firewood now?" Honey Bunch asked him. She did not see any around.

"Yes," Axel replied. "But I have to uncover it first."

Near a big tree was a great heap of snow. To the visitors' surprise, Axel began brushing off the top snow. Underneath was a pile of logs.

One by one Axel lifted the logs down and piled them onto the sled. The girls offered to help him, but he said he could do it alone. When the sled was full the boy tied the logs fast. Then he said:

"I can't turn around here, so I'm going to drive in a wide circle. Suppose you girls go back the way we came and I'll meet you down by the road."

Since the pony was such an expert on snowshoes, he and Axel were waiting for them when they arrived at the road. As the children came out of the forest they were surprised to see that it was snowing again. Before they reached the cabin it was coming down very hard.

"Maybe you'll have to stay all night," said Christina. "If the storm gets too bad you won't be able to drive back to Snowtop Inn."

This was exactly what happened. The Mortons waited all afternoon, hoping the storm would let up so they could start out. But it grew colder and colder. The wind howled and blew the falling snow round and round.

"I'm so delighted to have you stay," said Mrs. Vasa kindly. "Now we can have a real Swedish evening."

142

"What's a Swedish evening?" Stub asked.

Mrs. Vasa smiled. "You shall see. First I shall cook part of the dinner in the open fire-place."

"Please make some fish pudding," Christina begged her mother.

"And custard with *lingon*," Axel requested. He explained that *lingon* is the Swedish word for cranberries.

When dinner was ready they all sat down by the big open fire. Mrs. Vasa heaped everyone's plate with the delicious food. The visitors declared Mrs. Vasa was the best cook they had ever known.

"Suppose we sing some songs for our visitors," her husband suggested when they finished eating. "I'll explain in English what they mean."

Honey Bunch and Stub listened intently as Axel, Christina and their mother and father sang the pretty songs. Honey Bunch liked best the one about God watching over little children.

> *With God no one is safer*
> *Than the children He loves.*
> *Not the birds in their nests*
> *Nor the stars up above.*

When bedtime came the three little girls went to Christina's room. Christina shared her big bed with Honey Bunch, and Stub slept on a cot. The day had been a busy one for the Morton children, and they soon fell asleep.

The next morning the sun was shining again, and as soon as breakfast was over, Daddy said his little family should leave at once. Axel hooked up Mountain King and brought him to the door. The horse stepped along in lively fashion, pulling the cutter and its passengers through the heavy snow.

"It's awfully deep," said Honey Bunch, "and we haven't any tracks to follow. You know the way, don't you, Daddy?"

Her father assured her he did, but after they had driven half an hour she noticed a frown on his forehead. Finally she asked him if anything was wrong.

"I hate to admit it," Mr. Morton replied, "but I'm afraid I got off the road to Snowtop Inn."

"We're on some road, aren't we?" Stub asked.

"I'm not even sure of that," her uncle answered. "The snow is so deep it's hard to tell. I believe I'll turn around and go back to some familiar point."

He pulled on the left rein, and Mountain King made a complete circle. Back and back they went, but none of the Mortons could see anything they recognized. There was not a house in sight, and no one came along in a sleigh to direct them.

"What are we going to do?" Stub said after a while. She was beginning to be frightened.

"I guess we'll just have to keep on until we come to a house," her uncle replied.

But they did not come to a house, and finally he stopped.

"I'm going to get out and walk back a ways," he said. "I think I saw the top of a road sign in the snow."

After he had gone, Mrs. Morton discovered that a scarf she had worn around her neck was gone. She and the children looked in the sleigh for it, but it was not there.

"It must have been blown away by the wind," she said, "but it can't be far away, or I would have missed it before."

Honey Bunch stood up and looked back. She thought she could see her mother's scarf off to one side of the road. She offered to get it.

"No! No!" said her mother. "The snow is too

145

deep. You girls stay here in the sleigh. I'll get the scarf."

Honey Bunch and Stub sat down again. At this moment Mountain King snorted.

"What made him do that?" Honey Bunch asked her cousin. Since Stub lived on a farm, Honey Bunch thought she ought to know.

"I guess those birds made him do it," her cousin answered.

A whole flock of birds had landed on the snow near the cutter. They pecked and pecked, trying to uncover berries on the snow-covered bushes. But the children could see that the birds were not going to find anything. Suddenly Honey Bunch had an idea.

"If we shoo the birds away, I'm sure they'll lead us to a house."

"Why?" Stub asked.

"If the birds can't find anything to eat here, they'll fly to a house and get some seeds," she said wisely.

Stub agreed. The two little girls cried "Shoo! Shoo!" at the top of their lungs, and clapped their hands loudly.

At once the birds flew away. But something else happened also. The children had frightened Mountain King and he started to run. The cousins sat down very suddenly on the seat of the cutter. Stub grabbed the reins, but she was not able to stop the horse.

Honey Bunch clung to her side of the cutter. Both girls shouted: "Whoa! Whoa!"

Stub kept pulling hard on the reins, and finally Mountain King seemed to be slowing down a little bit. But just then the right runner of the sleigh hit something at the side of the road.

The sleigh tilted. Honey Bunch lost her hold and was thrown out headfirst into the deep snow!

CHAPTER XIII

LOST ON THE MOUNTAIN

"Oh!" screamed Stub, who had been able to stay in the cutter.

The sleigh righted itself, and she pulled even harder on the reins. Finally Mountain King stopped.

Mr. and Mrs. Morton had seen the accident. They started to run toward the spot where Honey Bunch was lying in the snow. But before they could get to her, the little girl picked herself up and began brushing the snow from her face.

"Are you all right, dear?" her mother asked anxiously.

"I can't see," Honey Bunch wailed.

It was no wonder. The poor child's face was covered with snow. Mrs. Morton pulled out her handkerchief and wiped it off.

Daddy Morton had gone to look after Stub and Mountain King. He climbed into the cutter, took the reins, and drove back. By this time, Mrs. Morton had managed to brush all the snow from Honey Bunch and found she was not hurt.

"We'd better get started now," Mr. Morton said. "But I admit I don't know which way to go to reach the Inn."

He had not found a road sign. The post he had seen was merely a stake driven into the ground to show how deep the snow was. Honey Bunch suggested following the birds, saying they might be going to some house for food.

"I believe your idea is a good one," Daddy said. "I'll try it."

He turned the sleigh around and went back to a crossroad. Then he went in the direction which the birds had taken.

It was not until Honey Bunch had been riding for some little time that she began to feel a trickle of water down her back.

"I'm melting inside," she said, squirming.

Mother laughed and said some snow must have got inside her suit and melted.

It was not long after this that they saw a big building ahead.

"It's Snowtop Inn!" cried Honey Bunch. "Oh, Daddy, the birds brought us home!"

Everyone was glad to be back. Mr. Morton let his passengers off and drove the cutter to the stables. Several people in the lobby of the hotel hurried up to Mrs. Morton and the children. Everyone had been worried, and all were glad to see them back safe.

Miss Allen and Billy met them just as they were stepping into the elevator. The hostess said she had missed the children very much, and had been afraid they might have been lost in the storm the day before.

"We didn't get lost until this morning," Honey Bunch told her. "We stayed with Christina all night and had lots of fun."

"We had a real Swedish evening," added Stub.

"I'm glad you're all right," said Billy. "I was looking everywhere for you. I wanted to tell you something."

He explained that there would be a very special surprise in the children's dining room that evening, and that Honey Bunch and Stub should be sure to eat there.

"I don't know what it is," he said, "but my Aunt Dorothy does."

Miss Allen laughed and said it was a big secret and she would not tell it.

"Oh, I like secrets," said Honey Bunch. "We'll be there."

She and Stub decided to put on their prettiest dresses. They had been saving them for a special occasion, and this seemed like just the right time to wear them. Stub's was bright yellow and had a little jacket. Honey Bunch's was pink and had lace on the collar and sleeves. Whenever she wore this dress, Honey Bunch always put a little butterfly pin in her hair.

When they were dressed, the cousins hurried down to the children's dining room. They found seats near Betty and Sammy, who wanted to hear all about how they had been lost in the snow. Honey Bunch and Stub told the story all over again.

"I'd have been awfully scared," said Betty.

It was not until the end of the meal that the big surprise came. Suddenly the lights went out and the pantry door opened. In came Wilbur, the chef, as usual wearing his high white hat and pushing his cart.

On the cart was a great white castle with many, many windows. And all the windows were lighted up!

"It's beautiful!" cried Honey Bunch.

151

The chef did not tell the secret of the castle until he stopped the cart in the center of the floor. Then he pulled a long knife from a drawer in the cart, and cut one turret right off the castle!

"It must be a cake!" exclaimed Stub.

The little girl had guessed correctly. Only it was not like a regular cake. It was hollow in the center so the light could fit inside. One by one the chef cut off sections of the castle, and when the lights in the room went on, waitresses passed the pieces to the children.

"I have the king's bedroom," said Sammy gleefully.

"I have the queen's," laughed Betty.

Honey Bunch and Stub could not decide which parts of the castle they had. What they did know, though, was that the cake tasted delicious. Honey Bunch, thinking of what her mother often said about Mrs. Miller's cakes, remarked:

"It's as light as a feather!"

The boys and girls thought the castle was to be the only surprise of the evening. But just as they finished eating the wonderful dessert, Miss Allen rose to make an announcement. She tapped a spoon against her tumbler to attract everyone's attention.

"Please, will all of you listen carefully?" she asked. "Day after tomorrow at four o'clock there will be a special dancing party. I'd like all of you to come. We shall have it in the big ballroom."

The children were delighted to hear this, and began to say "Oh" and "Ah" and "Won't that be fun!" Miss Allen had to tap on her glass again for them to be quiet.

"Now, I'd like each boy here to ask a girl to be his partner," she said, smiling. "I'm sorry there aren't as many boys as girls at Snowtop, but that won't matter. The rest of the girls may dance together."

She went on to say that after the boys had chosen their partners, they were to talk over with them the kind of dance they would like to do together. They could wear fancy costumes or not, but their dance was to be interesting for other people to watch. No doubt many grown-ups would come to look at them.

Stub leaned over to Honey Bunch and whispered, "This must be the party Billy Allen is going to ask you to."

153

She was thinking of the time when she and Honey Bunch had gone down the back stairway of the Inn and had heard Billy and his aunt talking. Billy had said he wanted to ask Honey Bunch to be his partner the day of the big party.

"Maybe," Honey Bunch agreed.

She hoped this was true, because Billy was a very good dancer. She was sure they could think up something nice to do together. After supper, when Sammy Simms came up to her and asked if she would be his partner, she said:

"Well, thank you, Sammy, but I'm afraid I can't."

The little boy guessed that someone else already had asked her, and went off to find another partner. Honey Bunch wished that Billy Allen would hurry up and come to speak to her!

In the meantime a lad by the name of Johnny Scattergood, who was full of fun, had asked Stub to be his partner. They sat down in a corner of the dining room to talk about the dance they would do. They decided they wouldn't have any fun being fairies or dolls, so what could they be?

"I guess we'd better be clowns," Stub giggled, and Johnny thought this was a good idea.

154

"My mother can make me a costume," he said. "I'll ask her to make a red one. What color do you want?"

"Maybe I'd better have black," Stub laughed. "I always fall down and get dirty. Then it won't show."

"Say," said Johnny, as a sudden thought came to him. "Why don't we have that for our clown dance? You fall down first and I'll fall over you. Then you get up and fall over me."

By the time the two children had planned the clown dance, they were laughing so hard that tears rolled down their cheeks. They could hardly wait for the day after tomorrow. When Stub entered her room she flopped down on her bed, still laughing.

Honey Bunch, however, did not feel very happy. Billy Allen had not come to ask her to be his partner. She had refused Sammy, and she was sure that by this time all the boys had asked other girls to be their partners. She knew that if she were to be in the entertainment at all, she would have to dance with another girl.

"Probably what I heard Billy say had nothing to do with this party," she thought. "I was silly not to be Sammy's partner."

Honey Bunch decided not to let anyone know she felt bad. She asked Stub why she was laughing so hard. When her cousin told her, she too laughed at the thought of the two clowns falling over each other.

"I 'spect you'll be all black and blue if you fall down too many times," said Honey Bunch. "You'd better practice how to fall down and not hurt yourself."

"How can you do that?" asked Stub.

Honey Bunch thought she remembered how it could be done. Her teacher in dancing school at home once had shown her pupils how to fall without hurting themselves. Now she tried to show Stub. But something was not quite right. After Honey Bunch had received several hard bumps, she decided not to try it any more.

The little girls slept soundly and woke up early the next morning. Directly after breakfast they went to the children's skating pond where Mitzi, the daughter of the skating instructor, was to give them a lesson. As they were sitting on the bank, putting on their skates, Susan Jane Black came over to them. She did not say "Hello" or "Good Morning" or anything like that. Instead, she said:

"Who asked you girls to the dance tomorrow?"

Honey Bunch's face turned very red and she did not answer. Stub spoke up and said Johnny Scattergood had asked her. But she did not tell Susan Jane what their dance was going to be.

Honey Bunch put her skates on very quickly and started off. Susan Jane stopped her.

"You didn't tell me who asked you to the dance tomorrow," she said. "I'll bet nobody did. Well, I'm going to have the best dancer in the place," she bragged. "Billy Allen asked me."

"That's very nice," said Honey Bunch. She could hardly keep from crying. "Come on, Stub," she said, and skated off to where Mitzi was waiting for them.

Honey Bunch had a very good time and did not see Susan Jane again until late that afternoon. Mrs. Morton and Stub had been working on the clown costume, and Honey Bunch had gone off with her daddy. But now the little cousins were playing together once more in the snow.

"Let's go over and see what those children are doing," Honey Bunch suggested.

157

Several children were playing tag. Among them were Billy Allen and Susan Jane. Just as Honey Bunch and Stub reached them, Susan Jane said she was tired of playing tag and had thought of something wonderful to do.

"What is it?" cried one of the boys.

Susan Jane asked if they had ever dug in the sand at the seashore. All the children said they had.

"Well, let's dig a pit in the snow," Susan Jane suggested. "Then somebody can lie in it and we'll heap snow over him the same way we do sand."

Everyone except Honey Bunch thought it was a good idea. She said it would be too cold. Susan Jane looked at her, annoyed.

"You stay out of this if you're so afraid," she said.

Honey Bunch said no more, and the other children began to dig a pit in the snow. When Susan Jane asked who wanted to be covered up with snow first, Stub offered. Her cousin tried to keep her from doing it, but Stub thought it would be fun.

"I'm willing to be covered too," said Billy Allen, and he lay down on the snow by Stub.

158

At once all the children except Honey Bunch began heaping snow over the two on the ground. It made her feel funny inside to see it, so she wandered off to watch some men cutting ice on a pond not far way. Their horses were working on the ice with them. Honey Bunch thought it was wonderful the way the horses stood right on the ice. They had potato sacks tied over their hoofs to keep them from slipping.

The men had big saws. After they cut out a big block of ice, they put a chain around it and the horses dragged it to the shore.

After watching them for a few minutes, the little girl went back to see how the snow game was getting along. She found that Stub had asked the children to stop covering her because she was getting cold.

They had removed the snow, and Stub was just getting to her feet. Many of the boys and girls were tired of the game and went off. But the three that were left heaped still more snow over Billy Allen and patted it down tightly.

"You're right up to his neck!" cried Honey Bunch. "He'll be sick! Please don't put any more snow on him!"

Susan Jane gave the little girl a push. She

insisted Billy was all right, and that Honey Bunch did not know what she was talking about.

"I do feel sort of cold," said Billy.

"Oh, don't be a sissy!" cried Susan Jane. "Honey Bunch, you always want to spoil everything!" she added. "Why don't you go up to the hotel and play with the cat?"

Suddenly Billy Allen's face began to grow white.

"Oh!" Honey Bunch exclaimed. "Something is the matter with Billy. We must get him out right away!"

When Susan Jane looked at him she too became frightened. Quickly she and the other children began to dig at the snow which covered Billy. But the snow had packed, and it was too hard for them to dig away with their hands.

CHAPTER XIV

HONEY BUNCH'S DISCOVERY

THERE were no grownups around to help Billy Allen. Suddenly Honey Bunch thought of the men she had seen cutting ice. Running as fast as she could, slipping and sliding, falling down and picking herself up again, she finally came to the pond.

"Help! Help!" she cried.

The men looked up and asked her what was the matter.

"A boy's stuck in the snow!" Honey Bunch said excitedly.

The ice cutters did not wait to hear any more. One of them leaped onto the back of a horse. The second one picked up Honey Bunch and flung himself onto the other animal.

"Show us the way!" the man cried, and the little girl pointed her finger.

Like the wind they raced to Billy Allen. When they reached the place where he lay covered, the men got to work at once. With their

strong fingers and their heels, they dug away
enough snow to lift the poor boy out.

One of the men jumped onto a horse, took
Billy in his arms, and rode off quickly to the
hotel. Honey Bunch and the other children
followed as fast as they could, but by the time
they reached Snowtop Inn, Billy Allen already
was in his room being treated by a doctor.

Many of the guests at the Inn were sad that
evening when they learned what had happened
to Billy. They were told he would be in bed for
several days.

This did not suit Susan Jane at all. All she
could think about was that the boy would not be
able to be her dancing partner at the party the
next afternoon.

"That means I shan't have any fun at all," she
told herself crossly. "I don't want to stay at this
old hotel any longer."

The selfish little girl went to her parents and
begged them to leave Snowtop Inn. Mr. and
Mrs. Black, embarrassed over their daughter's
actions at the hotel, decided to leave early the
next morning.

The Blacks had gone by the time Honey
Bunch and Stub came down to breakfast, but the

children heard about it a little later from Santa Ross. He had driven Susan Jane and her parents to the station. The sleigh driver said he was glad they had left.

"Now we can have some peace around here," he remarked. "That Susan Jane—she's a corker. Why, you know, Billy Allen told me he was all ready to ask another little girl to the dance, but Susan Jane wouldn't give him a chance. She just up and insisted he take her!"

"Who was the other little girl?" Stub asked without thinking.

Santa Ross did not know, but he hoped she had another partner. Honey Bunch was afraid her cousin might tell something more. She pulled her away, saying Stub was supposed to have a fitting on her clown costume.

The children went up to their bedroom where Mrs. Morton was sewing. She told them it would be much easier to put the clown suit together right on Stub. But Stub did not seem interested. She was very absent-minded, and finally asked Honey Bunch if she would be the model.

"But I'm smaller," her cousin objected. "The clown suit will be too tight for you if it fits me!"

163

"I have to go on an errand," said Stub. "A very special errand. I can't tell you what it is until after a while."

She ran from the room, promising to be back soon. Honey Bunch wondered why her cousin was so mysterious. She tried on the suit for the party, and it made her feel sorry for herself all over again. She had no costume and no partner for the dance.

"But I mustn't care," Honey Bunch told herself. "I'll do something else. I'll get Daddy and have some fun and forget all about it."

When her mother was finished with the fitting, Honey Bunch put on her snowsuit and ran outside to find her father. He was watching the skaters.

"Daddy," she said, "would you take me for a drive this morning?"

"Yes, indeed," he said. "Would you like to go with the Eskimo dogs?"

"No," Honey Bunch replied. "I'd like to go in the sleigh with Mountain King."

"Where to?"

The little girl looked up at her father and smiled. "I'd like to go to the place where I fell out of the cutter."

164

"So you can see the deep hole you made in the snow?" Daddy teased her.

Honey Bunch had not thought of this. She recalled that her mother had been looking for her lost scarf when the sleigh had tipped and spilled Honey Bunch into the snow. After that everyone had forgotten about the scarf and gone back to the Inn.

"I want to look for Mother's scarf," Honey Bunch said.

"All right," Mr. Morton agreed. "We'll go to the stables and ask Santa Ross if he'll let us have the horse."

The jolly man was glad to let the Mortons take the cutter and Mountain King again, but he warned them not to get lost this time. Daddy was sure he knew the way, and he did drive straight to the place. It did not seem so far to Honey Bunch as it had the day before.

"I certainly got way off the road," Mr. Morton remarked, slowing down so they could look around for the scarf.

They did not see it anywhere. Finally they concluded the wind must have carried it far away.

"We're past the spot where Mother missed the

165

scarf, so I'm sure we're not going to find it," said Daddy.

"This is where I fell out!" Honey Bunch cried suddenly. She could see the hole in the snow. "Why do you s'pose our sleigh tipped over, Daddy?"

"Probably the runner hit some ice hidden under the snow," her father answered.

"I want to see it," said Honey Bunch.

She jumped from the cutter and began kicking away the snow. At first this was easy, but suddenly her little boot knocked against something very hard. It made her toes sting.

Looking down, she saw a dark object buried in the snow. Honey Bunch knew it was not ice. She tried to lift it, but she could not move it.

"Oh, Daddy, I've found something!" she cried. "And it isn't ice. Please come and pick it up!"

Mr. Morton stepped out of the sleigh and bent over to pull up the heavy object. But he could not budge it.

"I guess it's frozen fast," he said.

He worked for a long time before he could get the thing loose. Then he brushed the snow from it.

"What is it, Daddy?" Honey Bunch asked.

"A box," he replied. "It's locked, and there's no name on the box. I'd say there's probably money inside, or possibly jewelry."

Jewelry! Honey Bunch stared at her Daddy when she heard this.

"Maybe it's Mr. Vasa's lost jewelry!" the little girl cried out.

CHAPTER XV

LEAVING WINTERLAND

WHEN Honey Bunch said the box might belong to Mr. Vasa, it was her daddy's turn to stare in surprise. His little daughter might be right! Maybe she had found the jewelry which the messenger said he had lost!

"We'll find out right away," said Mr. Morton. "Hop in, my dear, and I'll drive to Mr. Vasa's cabin at once."

Honey Bunch was so excited she could hardly sit still. It seemed like such a long ride to the jeweler's home, but actually it did not take Mountain King many minutes to get there. The horse seemed to sense something important was going on and trotted swiftly along the road.

Christina heard the sleigh bells and ran out of the house. She was glad to see her friends, but was somewhat surprised.

"Is your Daddy at home?" Honey Bunch asked quickly. "We have something to show him."

"Yes, I'll get him."

As the Mortons stepped from the sleigh, Christina hurried off to call her father. The jeweler came out at once, and Honey Bunch tried to tell him about the box. But she was so excited the little girl got everything mixed up.

"We have your pins," she said. "I mean, we found a box. Maybe your money's in it. No, I mean the things you lost."

Finally she gave up what she was trying to say and pointed to the box on the floor of the sleigh instead. Mr. Vasa took one look and exclaimed:

"It's mine! My lost box of jewelry! Oh, where did you find it, Mr. Morton?"

"I didn't," said the lawyer. "Honey Bunch found it."

"Oh, how can I ever thank you!" Mr. Vasa cried.

He pulled Honey Bunch to him and hugged her. Then the man insisted the Mortons come inside and tell him all about it.

The jeweler found a key to the box. Because the lock was so rusty, he could not open it at once. But when he did, the little girl gasped. Inside the box were rows and rows of beautiful

169

silver pins and rings. They were tarnished, and the velvet lining was water-soaked, but still the jewelry was beautiful.

"Did you make them all from snowflake designs?" Honey Bunch asked.

"Yes, and you can see each one is different."

Mr. Vasa told her and Mr. Morton that two more boxes were missing. But now that one had been found, maybe he would find the others near the same place.

"Then the messenger didn't keep them," Honey Bunch said.

"Probably not," the silversmith agreed. "I shall go down to that place where you found this box and look for the others."

Honey Bunch was just about to say she hoped they were buried in the snow, when she heard sleigh bells. Looking out of a window, she saw a familiar face.

"It's Santa Ross!" she cried, and ran to open the door.

"Well, well, so this is where you came with Mountain King," the jolly man said. "I'm glad you didn't get lost."

"It's a good thing we got lost last time," Honey Bunch told him, and explained about

170

finding the box containing Mr. Vasa's jewelry.

Santa Ross was very pleased indeed to hear this. He had never believed the young messenger had taken the jewelry, and he was glad to learn the truth. The sleigh driver pulled a letter from his pocket, saying it was for Axel.

"It's an invitation," he announced.

"Invitation?" repeated the boy, coming forward and taking the letter.

He opened it quickly and read the message. Honey Bunch noticed that Axel was blushing.

"What does it say?" his mother asked.

"There's going to be a party at Snowtop Inn this afternoon," he replied. "Christina and I are invited."

"How nice," said Mrs. Vasa. "What kind of party is it?"

Her son said it was a dancing party. Then shyly he added that Miss Allen wanted him to dance for them.

"Oh, you and Christina can do a Swedish dance together!" Honey Bunch cried.

"I can't do them very well," Christina said quickly. "Mama says I take after Papa."

Mr. Vasa laughed and declared his daughter was right; she was not much of a dancer. But

171

Axel was a good dancer like his mother. The boy smiled and looked again at the letter.

"Miss Allen wants me to dance with Honey Bunch," he said. "Will you be my partner?" he asked her.

Honey Bunch suddenly felt very happy. Now she would have a partner at the party!

"I'd love to," she said sweetly. "But I'm afraid I don't know any Swedish dance well enough."

"You did one in our barn the other day," Christina told her. "Remember?"

"Let me see you dance, Honey Bunch," said Mrs. Vasa.

The little girl did a few steps around the room. Mr. Vasa put a record on the phonograph, and Axel took her hand. In a minute they were dancing round and round.

"Oh, that is very good!" said Mrs. Vasa. "Only one thing is wrong, Honey Bunch. Watch! I will show you."

Honey Bunch had missed a few steps on a turn, but when she saw Axel and his mother do it, she knew how. After that she did the dance very well.

Christina had gone off to her bedroom. Now

she returned with a lovely Swedish costume for Honey Bunch to wear.

"Take this with you," she said.

"Oh, it's pretty!" exclaimed Honey Bunch, thanking her. "But won't you need it for the party?"

"No, I'm going to wear an American dress," laughed Christina.

Mr. Morton looked at his watch and said he and his small daughter should start back to Snowtop Inn at once if she was to attend the party. Axel and Christina said they would see them later.

As soon as Honey Bunch reached the hotel, she went to find Stub. All the way home she had been thinking about how her cousin had gone on a mysterious errand that morning.

"Stub," she said, "did you tell Miss Allen to invite Axel?"

The other little girl hung her head and would not answer at once; but finally she owned up that she had talked to Miss Allen.

"I knew Billy couldn't dance, and somebody ought to take his place," she explained. "And you are the best dancer at Snowtop, so you ought to have a partner."

This was a long speech for Stub, and she was out of breath when she finished.

"Oh, Stub, you're so nice," Honey Bunch said, kissing her cousin.

The little girls were very happy as they dressed for the party. When they went downstairs in the elevator, several people remarked about their costumes. They said Stub looked as funny as could be in her clown suit, and Honey Bunch as sweet as the roses on her Swedish costume. The little girl thought if Mrs. Miller the laundress were there, she would have said, "Sweet as sugar."

The ballroom was decorated with streamers of pink and blue paper. An orchestra was playing, and some of the guests were dancing. Around the sides of the room sat the grownups. Stub wondered why they had to come, and said so to Honey Bunch.

"I guess it's 'cause every show has to have people to look at it," her cousin answered after a moment.

Axel and Christina soon came in and joined them. Then Johnny Scattergood ran across the room to be near Stub. He looked like a real clown. Axel was very handsome in a red and white satin suit. He wore a little hat with a tassel.

When it was time for the youngsters to put on their show, Miss Allen got up to announce the dance numbers. She started by saying she was glad to report that her nephew Billy was very much better and would be out of bed in a couple of days.

"Oh, I'm so glad!" Honey Bunch whispered to Stub.

The clown dance was the first one on the program. Johnny and Stub did it very well, and when they got to the part where they kept getting in each other's way and falling down, the children screamed with laughter.

Honey Bunch's turn came near the end of the program, and when the dance was over everyone clapped. She and Axel had to bow several times, and finally Miss Allen asked them to repeat it.

"Oh, you were the best of all!" Christina exclaimed, when her brother and Honey Bunch came back to her.

"But Stub and Johnny made the children laugh the most," said Honey Bunch generously.

At the end of the party, Axel said he and

Christina would have to leave very soon as their father wanted them to get home before dark.

"My father asked me to tell you that he found the other two boxes of jewelry in the snow."

"Goody! Goody!" cried Honey Bunch. "Oh, Daddy," she said, as her parents walked over to her, "the messenger didn't take any of the jewelry. Mr. Vasa found it!"

"I'm glad to hear that," said the lawyer. "And I have some news too. The bad men who were copying Mr. Vasa's jewelry and selling it have been found. They won't make any more of it!"

"Oh, Papa will be so happy," said Christina. Then she looked at her brother. "Axel, we'd better go. Where's our bag?"

"Over there."

The boy went to get it. From inside he pulled out three packages. He handed one to his sister, and she in turn gave it to Honey Bunch. It was a beautiful Swedish doll.

"Please put it with Eleanor and the Oriental doll and all your others," Christina said. "Stub, I'm sorry you don't like dolls."

Stub was sorry in a way that she did not care more for dolls. This one was so pretty.

176

"Thank you very much, Christina," Honey Bunch said, holding the lovely new doll close to her.

Axel handed a small package to Stub and one to Honey Bunch, saying they were from Mr. Vasa. Eagerly the little girls opened them and found two exquisite silver pins inside! Honey Bunch's was made from the snowflake design of the six dancing fairies, and Stub's pin had a pretty pattern of stars all in a cluster.

"They're wonderful!" cried Honey Bunch. "I wish—I wish your daddy were here, so I could give him a big hug."

After the Vasa children had gone, Honey Bunch told her father and mother she was sure she never would meet such lovely children again. But of course she did. You may hear all about them in: "HONEY BUNCH: HER FIRST TRIP TO THE BIG WOODS."

"My work here is finished," said Daddy Morton a little later. "Tomorrow we must go back to Barham."

Honey Bunch and Stub were sorry to leave the Inn, for they had had a wonderful vacation. They had to get up very early to catch the morning train. But the children enjoyed the drive to

177

the station through the crisp morning air with Santa Ross. The two little girls sat up front with him.

"Be sure to come again next year," he said.

"We will if we can," they told him.

When they reached the station, Honey Bunch did not take her eyes from the man. Even when the big train rolled in, she continued to stare at him.

"Good-bye!"

"Good-bye!"

The children climbed aboard and found seats. Honey Bunch looked from the window to watch Santa Ross drive away.

"Why did you look at him so much?" Stub asked her when the train started.

"Because I b'lieve I'll never see anybody again who looks so much like Santa Claus," Honey Bunch replied. After a little while she added, "And I'm sure I'll never get so near the top of the world as I did at Snowtop."

THE END

178